ROSE

A New Tale, Book One

Madeline Simpkins

This is a work of fiction. Names, characters, places, and incidents either are the product of the author's imagination or are used fictitiously, and any resemblance to actual persons, living or dead, businesses, companies, events, or locales is entirely coincidental.

ROSE
Book one of the A New Tale series

ISBN 978-0-9983981-0-5

Dedication

To Ella and Samantha.
I hope you both always love reading fairy tales

Table of Contents

Prologue

Mark Steed refused to sit by idly anymore. He slammed the door of his room shut behind him forcefully, causing the walls to shake slightly around him. Now his parents would know for sure that he was back...for the time being. He picked up a shoe that had been left on the floor and hurled it at the wall, but it bounced back with a dissatisfying thud as though it was mocking him.

Just moments ago, he had snuck through the back door of his house. It was early enough that his parents were still at the breakfast table, and he had done his best to be quiet. He had gotten close enough to hear them talking about him. He had been expecting this. After all, he hadn't come home in a couple weeks. He had been spending his time at a friend's house.

His mom was in the middle of asking his father when he thought Mark was going to be home. Mark had stared at the back of his father's chair hard, waiting for him to speak, but he never did. All his father did was take a long time to take another sip from his cup of coffee and turn the page in his newspaper. Finally, he gave a small shrug. Mark's eyes flashed and he decided that enough was enough. He was done with this place.

Now, as he moved things around in his closet looking for an old backpack, he felt the anger leaving. It left a huge hole that soon filled with sadness. How could they be so callous and uncaring to their own son?

Mark felt numb as he found his backpack and shoved some things into it. When he had all of the essentials, his bedroom looked like a tornado had touched down in the middle of it. He looked once more around at the room that he had lived in for years, before walking out. As he turned to leave, something stopped him. He hesitated for just a moment more before quickly grabbing an old picture. It was one of the only times that he remembered being truly happy with his parents. They had been on a cruise and were on a beach. They all had a good time then, but it was a long time ago. The picture had been taken when he was twelve.

The picture, frame and all, was soon buried at the bottom of the bag, and, once more, Mark was on his way out.

He made a quick detour to his parents' bedroom. Inside their closet was an old shoe box that held some valuables saved away for emergencies. One of these things was a debit card connected to a special account. Mark put it in his wallet.

He didn't hesitate anymore and walked determinedly to the front door. No one was going to stop him. He was finally going to get away from this place. Mark debated taking his car. On one hand, he didn't want to be tracked through the license plate, but on the other, he would be an idiot for not using it. Finally, he made up his mind to just go ahead and take it. His parents probably wouldn't go to the police for a while, since they hadn't when he had been gone for two weeks.

He drove for quite some time on backstreets around his house, planning what he was going to do in the next couple days. After a little while, he pulled over in front of a store. He paused for a brief moment before getting out and walking up to the ATM just outside its doors. He knew exactly what he had to do to get some cash, but it was nerve wracking to know that if he was caught, he could be arrested.

Mark pulled himself together and entered in a pin number and swiped the card. He thought for sure that someone would catch him as he forged his dad's signature. A few seconds later, the signature was given official approval, and Mark began to withdraw money from the account. He could only take out a certain amount of cash at a time. The process would have been boring if not for the fact that Mark's heart was beating fast enough for two people. Five minutes later, he had officially drained several thousand dollars.

Mark put the last of it in his backpack, got back in the car, and took a deep breath. He made a quick phone call to some friends. They would want to know where to meet him. There was a fast-food restaurant nearby where he could wait for them to show up. He got there, ordered some food, and sat down to wait. About half an hour later, they came in and joined him at the table. Both friends were tall and had an air of uneasiness about them, as though they were expecting someone to jump out at them from the crowd. Carter was the slightly shorter one with dark brown hair and brown eyes, while the other, Josh, was dirty blonde, like Mark, but with blue instead of green eyes. Anyone passing by would have just seen three teenagers meeting up for a meal.

Mark had known Josh and Carter for several months, and they all felt more than ready to put some distance between themselves and this town. He didn't know much about Carter, except that he was trying to hide from the foster care system. He had two years before he was on his own for good, and two years was a long time to wait. As for Joshua, Mark knew that he was smart but knew little about his home life. He suspected that it wasn't a pleasant one though.

Right before the boys sat down at his table, he passed them a twenty dollar bill.

"Get yourselves some food." When Josh hesitated to take the money, Carter rolled his eyes and grabbed it. As he moved to the counter to order, Josh lingered behind.

"Are you sure you're ready?" Josh stared at Mark, who nodded firmly, not giving himself a chance to hesitate.

"I've waited too long for this to happen. I'm ready." When Josh didn't move to join Carter in line, Mark raised an eyebrow. "You not gonna get anything?" Josh gave a small smile before sitting down.

"No. I've known Carter long enough to know that he'll order something for me." Mark gave a slight nod. Interesting. "Don't mind him right now." Josh continued. "He just got dumped by his girlfriend for the third time in a row." Mark gave a small chuckle. That explained it.

"Who was it this time?" Josh was shaking his head before Mark finished the question.

"No. It was the same girl all three times." Mark snickered.

"I'm guessing that you got enough cash." Carter walked up at that moment, oblivious to why Mark was laughing. Mark wiped the smile off his face and nodded to him.

"Yep. We're all set."

"Then I guess we're ready to hit the road." Carter paused. "Right after we get the food."

The boys quickly finished their food once it came and left the restaurant. As Brent got the car started, Carter quickly called shotgun.

"Who's car?"

"Mine." He probably thought that Mark had stolen it.

"Sweet."

5

They had been driving for almost half an hour outside the city limits, when they came to a bend in the road where one side was a straight drop into the ocean while the other backed into a cliff that was roughly fifty feet tall. Mark took a quick look at the ocean as he made the turn. He had barely looked away from the road before Carter shouted.

"Watch out!" Mark jerked his eyes back and managed to swerve just in time to avoid hitting an old woman in the middle of the road. He quickly slammed on the brakes and got out of the car.

"What were you thinking?! I could have killed you!" He shouted.

The woman had a huge blanket draped around her whole body, even though it was warm enough to not need one. She didn't look very old, maybe in her late thirties, but it was obvious she had seen better times. Mark heard Josh and Carter get out of the car. They all studied her tired form, shaggy greyish hair that obviously hadn't been washed in a long time, and her dirty complexion. She grimaced as she moved a couple of steps towards them. Mark shook his head slightly at the sight and began to walk back to the car door.

"Young men!" Mark paused and winced at the scratchy sound of her misused voice. "Would you be able to provide me with a ride to the next town?" Mark really couldn't believe that she would even suggest such a thing. Almost as though hearing his thoughts, the woman continued, "I don't have anything to offer you except for this flower." Mark turned his head to look at her as she reached a hand

6

into one of the folds of her blanket, and presented them with a rose. As far as the he could tell, the flower had appeared from nowhere, but it was very much real. The small flower was supported by a single stem, and was just preparing to blossom into its full glory. It was planted in a delicate glass pot, through which they could all see small glimpses of thin white roots.

Mark shifted his gaze to her face, slightly annoyed that the crazy woman was trying to get his money.

"No," he said coldly. "We don't have any money to give you." He abruptly turned and began to walking back to the car again. Josh and Carter passed a secret look to each other before following Mark's example, ignoring the old lady.

"Please, young men!" The woman called out to them once more. "I don't have anyone to go to and no way to get anywhere. Would you at least let me call for a cab on a phone and provide means to pay for it? I don't have the energy at this age..." Her voice broke as she finished her sentence, and she let out a hacking cough. "Please?" She attempted once more to ask them for help. "You can have the rose, even if you just point me in the right direction!" Mark turned suddenly, his eyes full of anger.

"Didn't you hear me?" He demanded. "I don't have anything to give you! Now go away!"

The woman slowly lowered the beautiful blossom and narrowed her slightly bloodshot eyes.

"So," she said calmly with a hint of sadness, her voice suddenly seeming more clear. "For someone with several thousand in his pocket, you won't even spare a few dollars for someone less fortunate than you?" She suddenly stood up straighter, going from barely over five feet tall to almost six feet tall, falling short of Mark's height by a few inches.

Mark immediately backed up, feeling at once as though he was in over his head. He tried to open the door to his car, but it wouldn't budge.

"All I asked of you was for a little help." The woman's voice grew even more youthful, and she took another step closer to the boys, who all immediately stumbled back, trying to keep distance between them and her. "I even resorted to pleading with you." Her grey hair suddenly turned a rich dark brown. All at once, when it had only just barely come to her shoulders, it fell almost to her waist, cascading down her back in soft curls. "All the while, I offered you the one thing I had that might be considered precious. A simple rose."

The blanket around her shoulders fell to the ground, revealing old sweatpants and a shirt that hung off of her awkwardly. But almost immediately after the boys took this in, a small ripple of light passed over her, causing the sweat pants to change into a soft sea blue, filmy skirt that was just barely longer in the back. The large shirt shrank, joining with the skirt to form a dress. The sleeves extended just past her shoulders, smooth against her now porcelain white skin. The neckline dipped gently in the front and back, lined with an almost invisible lace. At the very end of the dress, the color suddenly

8

changed into a deep ocean blue. The dress looked almost as if it was moving with a mind of its own as an invisible breeze slowly flowed around the woman.

A small sigh escaped the woman's pink lips. "Pride has been your downfall. For all of your sakes, I hope that you will learn this lesson you are soon to face." The last bit of transformation happened around her eyes, which changed from a dull brownish grey to a color that was impossible to pin down. Her eyes seemed to hold all of the colors of the rainbow at once, making it difficult for the boys to look directly at her face. She turned to Josh and Carter first.

"You did nothing to aid me, even though you knew in your hearts what was right. You must learn to become leaders by coming to another's aid. You will remain in an older form, until you can learn this lesson, which I fear will be a long and harsh journey." Josh and Carter opened their mouths, but before they could ask anything, the woman turned to Mark, who subconsciously took another step back. Her voice was full of sympathy as she spoke.

"You must learn to give up your selfishness and pride. As proof, you must learn to love someone, and in turn be loved by her. This lesson of yours will be the hardest to learn. In the past you have been loved for your appearance, but not for who you are. Your body will be changed and will be seen as frightening to many." She held out the not-yet-blossomed rose to him. "You will have until the last petal falls. If you have not yet learned to love another, you will remain the same as Joshua and Carter, forever hidden from mankind and locked inside a veiled form. They will be your access to the world."

The woman bowed her head, her forehead almost touching the rose bud. A few seconds passed, in which Josh, Carter, and Mark all began to back farther away slowly, but they stopped when a burst of throbbing light came from the rose. Suddenly, the woman looked up, and a brilliant light came from within her, a force throwing all of the boys back against the side of the cliff wall. At first, Mark felt resistance, but then he fell freely, watching as his world turned black around him.

~*~

The highlight of my week, maybe even my entire year, was the day Mark Steed stopped coming to school. I had known him for about half a year when he disappeared. No one knew where he had gone, but since there were no police investigations launched, I assumed that he had been transferred to a different school.

Most people were disappointed that he was gone, and it took a ridiculous amount of time for the school to recover. The football team had lost their star player, so they were desperate to find a replacement quarterback that was good enough. I felt sorry for how many games were lost that season. For the majority of the female population of the school, he became some kind of legend.

As for me, I couldn't help but sigh in relief that he was gone. Mark hated me. Sure, he was

10

adored by everyone, and for good reasons: he was top of the class, athletic, and handsome. Even the juniors and seniors saw him as a type of role model. The first time I saw him, my heart tripped over itself, and I could barely speak within a ten foot radius of him.

But, that was before he publicly humiliated me.

I was new to the school, had second-hand clothes, and lived in a dump of a house. I always lit up like a strobe light around him. He was bound to notice and, boy, did he ever.

Sometimes, he would turn at just the right moment and catch my eye. Before I could look away, he would wink and go back to whatever it was that he was doing as I blushed. I don't know how many times that happened before I started to hear the whispering and laughter that followed me down the halls. People began to call me "Firefly" as they kept track of how many times Mark could make me blush. Not long after the nickname, I discovered the rumors. I ran home crying that day. In my mind, I kept trying to rationalize with myself that it couldn't have been Mark who had started them, but nevertheless, I started guarding my feelings from him and everyone else. I guess the problem was that half of the rumors were either about my home life or about how no one cared about me, and most of those were pretty close to reality.

The very next day, Mark followed me to the park near my house, making sure no one was

11

around before he revealed himself to me. At first I was freaked out, but it didn't take long for him to calm me down. For the following hour, I was certain that he was the sweetest and most kind boy ever. A week passed in a similar fashion, and I slowly let my guard down around him.

The following week, he invited me to a party that was going to be at his house, and like any other fool, I accepted. I walked the twenty minutes it took to get to his house and arrived in casual wear, only to discover when the door was opened that everyone was dressed up casino-style.

"Looks like Firefly showed up." The boy who had opened the door sneered at me, but my eyes were fixed on Mark as he made his way through the crowd towards me. He had a look on his face that made me feel like dirt under his feet.

"What are you doing here?"

"You invited..." My voice trailed off. I should have known something like this was going to happen.

"Why on earth would I invite someone like you to a party?" He spoke loud enough that several people could hear him. They stopped what they were doing to come watch the show. A couple of mock gasps escaped from their lips at Mark's words.

"I see." I whispered meekly.

I turned to leave, but Mark grabbed my shoulder and pulled me farther inside the house, pushing the door shut behind me. That should have been my cue to run.

"Wait, wait, wait. There's no rush! Besides," He looked right past me and nodded, "the party is just about to get started." He let go of me and stepped back. I tried to turn and get out of the house, but that was when a huge bucket of paint was dumped on top of me. For the longest time, I stood frozen, as black paint got in my mouth and dripped all over my clothes, ruining them. When my brain registered what had happened, I heard giggles beginning to come from the crowd, I ran as quickly as I could to get out of the house. Just as I opened the door, another wave of paint hit me. This time red mixed in with the black as I made it past the doorway and down the steps.

Laughter came from behind me as I ran into the night, slipping on the slick grass outside. I let out several small gasps of air, tears joining the paint running down my face.

"Hey, Firefly!" I jerked my head up, panicked. There were four boys holding some kind of gun about fifteen feet away. My eyes darted wildly around. What were they thinking?! They wouldn't actually shoot me, would they?! Mark wasn't anywhere in sight, but I knew he must have planned this all along. I scrambled to my feet as they fired the first shot.

Pain blossomed in my left side, along with a spray of yellow. Paintball guns. I wouldn't be killed, but it would definitely leave a mark. Another shot hit me along my jawline before I could turn away. I took off at a full sprint, trying my absolute hardest to ignore the pain of being shot over and over.

13

The boys didn't pursue me as soon as I ran around the street corner, but I kept running at a full sprint until the adrenaline wore off a couple blocks later.

By that time, I had reached a small group of trees where I tripped over a large root, slammed into the ground, and sobbed. For the longest time, I stayed there on the ground. My whole body hurt and I felt multiple bruises forming along my back, sides, arms and legs, and even one on my jaw. I had been wearing a thin blouse, but that was now covered in black, red, yellow, orange, and blue paint.

I was physically aching, but the pain that Mark had caused by pretending to be my friend, only to turn on me, hurt far worse.

Ever since then, I could never trust him or his friends. I kept quiet and out of their way, not that it helped me much. Mark pretty much ignored me, but his friends showed the most sincere thoughtfulness by making sure that I would never forget them. They never hurt me too bad, but it got to the point where I hid from them as much as possible. No one with any sense at the school liked them much, so I usually had a small warning if one of them was headed my way.

I was more than relieved when Mark left school. The attention that his evil friends gave me dwindled down, and I was able to get by being mostly ignored. I became a wallflower, and I was alright with that.

After all, wallflowers didn't get hurt.

Chapter 1

Two Years Later

I leaned against the stone brick of the building behind me and let out a breath. Well, that was it. School was officially out for the summer. I let a smile slip onto my face as I began the walk home.

About ten minutes later, I sat down on a park bench just across the street from my house. No one played at the park much anymore. It was too old and rusted, and part of me wondered if it would ever be shut down by the city before it got too dangerous. As my thoughts drifted around, they finally settled on thinking of whether or not I could get a summer job. Anyone who did so much as glance at our house would know that we needed one.

Out of the corner of my eye, I noticed a police car driving up the road. It parked not fifteen feet from me. I watched as a man got out and walked up to my house. That didn't look good. The man knocked and the door opened to reveal someone who was definitely not my father. Of course, I recognized him. He was the landowner.

15

But why would the landowner be at my house? My father appeared next to him, and I relaxed a little, but not much. Something had to be wrong.

My thoughts were interrupted by a young man sitting down next to me on the bench. I didn't pay much attention, but it became hard to ignore him when he kept clearing his throat.

"Yes?" I turned towards him, tension in my voice. He had light brown hair and was carrying a clipboard.

"I don't mean to intrude, but I was wondering if you could answer a question for me. I'm taking a survey...." I began to tune him out and turned back toward the small group on my front porch. It looked a little heated. I turned back when I realized the young man had stopped talking.

"Uh, sorry. Um. What was your question?" I kept glancing at the porch.

"If you had a family member in trouble, say a brother or sister, how far would you be willing to go in order to keep them safe?" Something about the way the young man phrased the question made me turn sharply to stare at him.

"As far as I needed to go." I heard the shouting get louder and turned back toward the porch. My father was in a loud debate with the landowner, and it looked like the officer was trying to break it up. Suddenly it happened. My father turned around and socked the police officer right across the face. I let out a gasp and quickly stood up.

"But would you-" I cut the young man off from speaking any longer. How had he not seen what had just happened?!

"You'll have to excuse me." I ran across the street and reached the front porch just as the police officer finished handcuffing my father, who was struggling and shouting loudly. The officer looked as though he was in pain, and my father was not helping. I winced at his temper and spoke to the landowner.

"Mr. Commer, what happened?" I was familiar with the man and had never seen him look as serious as he did now.

"Young lady," he stared me in the eye, "your father just openly assaulted a police officer." I bit my lip.

"I understand that, but why?" I kept an eye on my father as he was led to the police car. Mr. Commer looked at me for a bit as though he felt sorry for me.

"I'm not sure if you are aware or not that the rent on the house has not been paid in several months. I've sent notices, and I can't keep ignoring it. The payment must be made." He took a deep breath, suddenly sounding a bit more sympathetic. "Look, I know it's not easy on you or your mother, but I can't wait any longer." The police officer was walking back to us now.

"Can you give me one more week?" He looked at me firmly. "Please, Mr. Commer! I only just found out about this, but if you give me a week,

17

then I'm sure that I can figure something out. Just a week!" I was literally begging him now.

Mr. Commer looked down for a moment before looking back at me and nodding.

"Oh, thank you!"

"One week." Mr. Commer held up a finger. "I can't wait anymore."

"Yes sir."

I watched as Mr. Commer talked with the officer for a little longer before the officer left.

"Miss Packer." Mr. Commer nodded to me, and I lifted a hand in response as he began to walk away. He only got a few feet farther before he stopped and turned back around. He looked a little uncertain as to what he was about to say, and that made me nervous. "Miss. Packer, is- is there anything wrong?" I felt a chill go up my spine.

"What do you mean?"

"Are you and your brother safe here? Is there anything that you should tell someone?" I gave him what I hoped was a reassuring smile.

"You don't need worry about anything, Mr. Commer. I know that my mom is sick right now, but she's on some new medicine that should start working in a couple of weeks." He shook his head.

"You know that's not all that I'm asking. With your father gone, for a hopefully short amount of time, will your family have enough income to support itself?" My smile became a little more strained. I knew that he meant well.

"We're fine Mr. Commer." He gave me one more small smile before he nodded once more and finally got in his car.

I looked back at the park, but saw no one. I waited for Mr. Commer's car to disappear around the bend before going inside.

Letting out a sigh, I closed the door and walked directly to my room to dump my stuff on my bed. In a small one story house, I didn't have to go very far.

This was a disaster! Dad was gone. Mom was sick. We were about to get kicked out of the house. And, on top of all that, Mr. Commer sounded worried enough to send CPS to check up on us. I heard the front door open and slam shut.

From the sound of it, my brother, Dan, was getting home from school. Dan was like the twelve year old boy version of my mom. They both shared the same dark blue eyes and light brown hair, and right now they were about the same height.

"Hey, Alli! Are you home yet?" That was Dan alright. I stood up and followed the sound of slamming cabinets to the kitchen. I stared at him for a little bit until he noticed me standing there. "Oh, there you are. Is there any food anywhere?" He went back to digging through the currently open cabinet.

"Hey, Dan. We need to talk." He shut the cabinet and turned to face me stiffly.

"What happened?" I guess I wasn't as good at hiding my emotions as I thought. I took a deep breath, trying to figure out how to tell him.

19

"Well, there is a chance that Dad won't be home for a little while." I explained what had happened just a few minutes ago. Dan stared at me for a moment before leaning back against the counter behind him.

"So what happens to us?" I gave him a small smile.

"Don't worry. I talked to Mr. Commer, and we struck a deal. We'll be alright." I hope.

Dan looked at me, only half believing my words.

"Come on." I jerked my head towards our parents' bedroom. "Let's go see Mom."

I went ahead and left, knowing he would follow. Sure enough, a couple moments later, he was standing in the doorway while I sat next to Mom. She must have felt my weight settle onto the bed because moments later, she opened her eyes. She smiled at the sight of us.

"Hey. How was your day?" She sat up in bed and looked at us. Dan and I exchanged looks and I took a deep breath.

"Mom, you may not like this." I told her what I told Dan, omitting anything about potentially losing the house in a week. Mom, of course, was devastated to hear about Dad. I waited until Dan left the room to tell her the rest.

"Mom, do you know of any calls we can make, favors people might owe us, or perhaps some sort of secret money stash?"

"Oh, Alli." Mom put a hand to the side of my face. "You shouldn't need to be worried about things like this at your age." Yeah, but I did worry.

Later that night, Dan was once more going through the kitchen cabinets while I sat at the table, trying to think up a plan to keep the house. A loud banging came from the front door, my head jerked up while Dan looked at me and froze. Banging at this time of night was never good news and often dangerous.

"Dan, get to your room." My tone didn't leave any room for argument. His eyes grew wider and for a moment he looked much younger than his twelve years.

"Do you think that...?" More banging interrupted him and I stood up.

"I don't know. Go to your room just in case. And close the door." Normally, he would have argued with me longer, but I think that something in my voice stopped him. He disappeared into his room as I went to the door.

I opened the front door just as someone's raised fist came down on it. My shoulder took the brunt of the force, luckily, and not my face. The person quickly pulled back when I gasped in pain.

There were two men standing there, looking impatient. Neither one bothered to apologize for my now very bruised shoulder. Some would probably call me an idiot for opening the door, but I was more worried about what would happen if I didn't answer the door.

21

"May I help you?" I hated how nervous my voice sounded as I spoke. I recognized the two men. They'd come over before to do 'business' with my father. I called one Rasp and the other Sile, mainly because I didn't know their names and one sounded like a pack-a-day smoker and the other almost never spoke.

"Yeah. Is Packer here?" The shorter of the two, Rasp, spoke up in his rough voice. They must have been looking for my dad.

"Not currently. I-" Rasp cut me off.

"Where is he, girl?"

"I'm afraid that he's been arrested-"

"You must be the daughter." He interrupted me again. I shifted nervously in place, not liking at all the way they were eyeing me. "You see," He leaned closer to the door frame, causing me to lean away, "Packer has a deal with us, and if he isn't here to fulfill his end of the deal, something might just happen." I was terrified, and wished that Dad was here. But, of course, he wasn't here when we needed him most.

"Hey, Alli." A man's voice came from behind me, which was definitely older than Dan's. I felt an arm slip around my shoulders, and I stiffened, glancing up to see a young man about twenty years old pull the door open farther. "Is something wrong?"

"No. They were just leaving." My voice sounded slightly strangled as I tried to work out what was going on. Rasp had backed off, and both of them looked suddenly wary.

22

"Okay, well, come on." He nodded his head back inside before bending down to whisper something in my ear. "Just act normal, everything's fine, although now would be a good time to blush." I immediately knew what he was talking about and a bright red flush crept up my face. I noticed that the two men on the porch looked both disappointed and slightly amused.

"Hey, no harm done." Rasp held up his hands and made his way down the porch steps, Sile following soon after. I shut the door quickly, as though that could get rid of them faster.

As soon as the door was shut, I threw the guy's arm off my shoulder and backed away.

"Who are you, and how did you get in?"

"Carter, and I had some help." He held out his hand, but I just narrowed my eyes at him.

"What help?"

"Uh..." Carter looked around as though searching for someone. He suddenly went into the kitchen, when I found Dan sitting at the table, looking slightly guilty. "This kid here helped me."

"Dan..." I couldn't believe this. My younger brother had just let in a complete stranger. A tapping came from the back door. Dan made to get up, but I stopped him.

"Stay." Normally, Dan wouldn't even pretend to have heard me, but I think something about the day's events stopped him. I went over and opened the door only to see the young man from earlier that day in the park. "You." I rubbed a hand over my face. "Come in." He walked in and sat down

23

next to Dan. "Now, will someone please tell me what is going on? Are you stalking me?" It was the only explanation I could think of at the moment.

"Um, no. Not really." Carter looked at me and then glanced quickly towards Dan, who was listening intently to everything around him.

"Hey Dan," I spoke softly. "I need to speak to these two alone for a moment." We had a small, miniature argument through a variety of glares. At last though, I won and he left in a huff.

When his bedroom door slammed shut, I turned back to Carter and...?

"Who are you?" I needed answers fast.

"Joshua."

"Right." I grabbed a seat directly opposite of him and waited for Carter to sit. "Explain. And this better be good."

"Well," Carter spoke. "from what we've gathered about your situation, you look like you could use some help." I stiffened, wondering how much he knew.

"What do you mean?"

"I mean, that I know how to help your family, but only if you agree to do something for us." There was no way that could imply anything good.

"How could you help?"

"We can't do anything for your father, but we can give you something that will cure your mom and we can solve your money problems." I was more on my guard than ever. How could they possibly know about all of that? Moreover, why were they doing this?

"What's in it for you."

"In exchange, you come with us." Whoa. Whoa. Whoa. What?!

"Come again?"

Carter attempted to rephrase his words. "If you come with us for the summer, we can-"

"No way!" I leaned back in my chair and almost fell over, suddenly a little freaked out. "If you guys think this is some sort of game-"

"No!" Joshua's face turned an interesting shade of red, and he suddenly sat up straighter, understanding why I was so freaked out. "You would come with us for the summer, but nothing would happen to you, especially not whatever you were thinking. I promise that you would be completely safe and nothing you didn't want would happen to you." I stared at them both for a little bit before shaking my head. Did they really think I was that stupid?

"No way-"

"Hey! Can I come back now?" Dan shouted from his bedroom and without waiting for a response, he walked back into the kitchen.

"Dan..." I stood up and glared at him, but he ignored me. He opened yet another cabinet, but closed it really fast, looking irritated. He held a mostly empty box of cereal, but I knew without even looking that there wasn't milk or yogurt in the fridge. I walked over next to him, wishing we were alone, without two strangers waiting to hear what we would say next.

25

.an you please find something in this
lat's edible? It doesn't even have to taste
Dan whispered harshly. I flushed when I
zed that this was exactly what Carter and
, nua could solve...if I went with them.

"Just eat it dry." I knew that I sounded tired.
"And please go back to your room. We're not done
in here." Dan rolled his eyes, but a few seconds
later, I heard his door slam shut once more. I leaned
against the kitchen counter, my back to Joshua and
Carter. The silence was very heavy. I couldn't very
well say that we would be fine, when they had seen
just how much food was in the house.

"Get out of here." I turned back around,
anger welling up within me. "Get out and don't
come back." I was expecting them to put up some
sort of fight, but they just stood up. Carter left first,
but Joshua remained a little longer. He pulled
something out of his pocket and set it down on the
table.

"Just in case you change your mind. Give
that to your mom, and she will get better." Who did
they think they were, some kind of magicians?

"Get out!" I hissed.

"But if it works?" I gave a harsh, skeptical
laugh. laugh.

"Then yes! I will come! Now leave!"

He left through the back door without a
word. The words I had just spoke rung in my head. I
had agreed. I hadn't meant to say that.

All that was left to show that the two young
men had been in my kitchen was a small vial that

26

held a light blue liquid. I stared at it for the longest of times before picking it up and going to my room. I dropped the vial into my desk drawer and pulled my small computer out. I had saved up forever in order to buy that thing off a teacher at school. It broke down a lot, which was probably why I had been able to get it for only eighty dollars, but it was still a lifesaver. Also, some neighbor had forgotten to put a password on their Wi-Fi, so I could do research from the comforts of my own home instead of traveling to the nearest coffee shop.

I began to research different chemicals, medicines, poisons, etc. that might be a light blue color, but no matter what I read, nothing shed light on what the liquid in the vial might be. There was a perfume-like odor that filled the room when I opened it, which didn't make any sense whatsoever. I put a drop of it on my finger, and, when it didn't burn a hole through my skin, I dabbed it on my tongue. My mouth felt a little warmer, but that feeling soon dissipated. Nothing. It didn't seem harmful in anyway. Did I trust it? No.

I glanced out of my room at the closed door of my parent's bedroom where Mom was sleeping once more. We had been to so many doctors, trying to figure out what was wrong with her, but nothing had helped. Steadily, the doctor bills had piled up, and now we just couldn't afford the help. I was scared that any day, we would need to go to the emergency room, but we would never be able to pay for it. What would happen then?

Steadily, Dad had grown more distant. He had gotten drunk several times and had slacked off on his job, until his company finally fired him. Sometimes, he would disappear for a week at a time, but he always came back, looking a little more defeated and a little more desperate. Now, he had been arrested, and there was no income whatsoever. There was an insane amount of debt, the house would be gone by the end of a week, and the family was falling apart. I couldn't pay for everything with only a couple of temporary jobs.

I looked at the vial in the drawer. It was well past midnight, and I really needed to get some sleep. At this point, no decision I made would be good.

~*~

I spent the next several days researching, trying to make up my mind on what I would do. At one point, I drove Mom down to the police department to speak with my father, but not much came out of that. I learned that there was an investigation going on about him, and some policemen would stop by within the next couple of days to look over the house for information. Great. By the time that I had gotten my mom home and returned the car I had borrowed from a neighbor, I was seriously considering giving Mom the vial of liquid in my drawer.

I went to my room and stared at the blue vial for the longest time before grabbing it. I hoped that this wasn't a mistake.

I woke Mom up and had her drink it. There was no immediate change, but I wasn't expecting any at all. I looked up to see Dan standing in the doorway. He was watching me silently with a strained look on his face. Standing, I walked with him to the kitchen.

"What was that?" Dan sat down at the table and put his elbows on his knees. "Was that the stuff those two guys gave you the other day?" I had given him less credit than he deserved. I didn't know he had known about the vial.

"Yeah."

"Will it work?"

"I don't know." I slid down the cabinets until I was sitting on the floor. "I just hope it helps."

There was silence for a moment.

"Will Dad be coming back?"

"I don't know." I wanted to speak more, but my throat had tightened too much. Tears fill my eyes and my breathing became more labored. I tried to take deep breaths, but I couldn't. "Dan!" It hurt to talk. I heard him open one of the cabinets. Moments later, he was holding a paper bag over my mouth.

"Breath, Alli! Come on. You can do this!" Dan did his best to calm me down, and after about ten minutes, my breathing began to come much easier.

"Thanks." I mumbled, pushing the bag away from my face. Dan sat back on his heels, relief flooding his eyes.

"Alli. We can't live like this. We need help." I knew that. What if that vial worked? What then?

"I know."

29

That night, I found it too hard to fall asleep with so many thoughts bouncing around my head. I wondered if Joshua and Carter were telling the truth or not, and if so, why they wanted me to go with them for the summer. If that didn't seem suspicious, then I don't know what did!

Still, I had made a deal. If by some crazy miracle, that vial had worked its magic, then Joshua and Carter might show up to make sure I held up my end of the bargain. That scared me.

I stared up at my ceiling. There were glow-in-the-dark stars everywhere. I made a wish on one. Maybe, if I was lucky, I would wake up in the morning and find that this had all been a dream.

Chapter 2

The next morning, I woke up to someone softly calling my name and shaking my shoulder. I groaned and turned over in my bed, giving a muffled protest. I heard soft laughing and suddenly tensed. There was only one person in this family who did that.

I sat up straight and stared at Mom directly in the eye. She had never gotten up before I did while she was sick.

"What-"

She gave a smile.

"Hey, I thought I'd surprise you."

I couldn't tell whether or not to be thrilled. Wait a moment. I suddenly remembered everything from yesterday. The deal I had made.

"Mom. How do you feel?" She looked a little surprised at the tone of my voice.

"I feel fine. I slept really well after the medicine you gave me last night and woke up feeling great! What type of medicine was that anyway?" I just stared at her for a moment, feeling as though I had just won the lottery, only to have the money stolen.

"I don't know. I gave it to you, but I didn't think that it would actually work, I mean, I..." My voice trailed off, taking large gulps of air in order to keep myself from hyperventilating. Mom grabbed hold of my shoulders.

"Alli. What is it? Look at me. What happened?" I looked at her until my breathing came under control.

"I made a deal." My voice had lost all of its emotion, and my mouth felt suddenly dry.

"What do you mean?" She was beginning to sound seriously worried.

"There were some men here yesterday. They made sure some of Dad's old business partners left and then they offered me a deal."

"Yes, I get that honey, but what do you mean? What was the deal?" I swallowed the lump in my throat and looked at the bed.

"They told me that they could make sure you got better and that the house and our money problems would be taken care of, but...but in return, I would spend the summer with them." Mom's eyes got wide, and I continued. "They said that I would be safe and that they wouldn't take advantage of me. They gave me that medicine. Said that if it worked on you, then I would go with them. And it worked." My voice cracked, and Mom wrapped me up in a hug.

"Listen. You do not in any way need to go. You are staying here if I have any say in this. Which I do." I gave a small smile.

"I love you."

32

"And I love you back."

~*~

When a knocking came from the door later that morning, I pulled it open and my smile slipped instantly from my face. Joshua was standing there, waiting.

"It worked, didn't it?" I opened my mouth to respond, but I couldn't make a sound.

"Alli? Who's at the door?" Mom came to the door behind me. When she saw Joshua, she frowned.

"What..." She trailed off.

"I see the vial worked."

Before I could say anything, Mom cut in. "Yes, it did. And there is no way that my daughter is going with you."

Joshua sighed a little as though he had been expecting this.

"I'm afraid that there will be a problem then."

"Oh? Explain." Mom's voice was cold. It was scary. I had never seen this side of her before now.

"You see, if Alli doesn't come with us, then the medicine stops working." I had never heard of something more ridiculous.

"Wait a second. You're telling me that the medicine will only work if I go with you. You must be crazy. This isn't some weird hocus-pocus." I shook my head slightly. He was crazy!

"Ok. Believe what you will, but when your mom gets worse as the day goes on, you'll know the reason."

33

Mom spoke up again. "Leave now."

Joshua left, but now there seemed to be a dark mood that settled over the whole house.

As I helped Mom in the kitchen, chopping up vegetables, my mind was in a completely different place. What if Joshua was right? What if Mom did relapse? My mind was so distracted that I forgot which way the knife blade was facing. It wasn't until I felt the blade biting into the palm of my left hand that I realized what I was doing.

I immediately jerked the knife away and cried out in pain as I cradled my hand to my chest. Mom hurried over when she heard me and tried to help me. I gritted my teeth at the pain, but when I saw that there was a lot of blood, I could feel my face drain of all color. Mom helped me sit down, and I put my head between my knees.

Eventually, the pain began to slowly fade into a dull throbbing. I washed my hands of the blood. It stung even more so as fresh blood came to the surface. It looked like the cut was deep and long, running all of the way across my palm. Mom put antiseptic on it and wrapped it up tightly. It wouldn't stop throbbing.

I kept glancing at Mom as she kept moving around, hoping that it was just my paranoia that made it seem like she was losing her energy rapidly. It wasn't until Dan spoke up after lunch that I realized that my eyes weren't fooling me. Mom hated admitting to it, but by the time early afternoon rolled around, she was back in bed, fast asleep.

I felt a hard lump in my throat. Joshua had been right. I closed my eyes as a couple tears slipped past. I grabbed a messenger bag and used my good hand to stuff several changes of clothes in it along with some family pictures. I had a feeling that Joshua or Carter would be back soon. I would be ready.

Sure enough, that evening, I opened the door once more to see Joshua standing there. Neither of us spoke for a moment.

"I'll get my bag." I whispered. Joshua nodded and pressed another vial into my hands.

"Here. Give this to her before you leave. It will work just like last time."

"Okay."

I made sure that mom took what was in the vial. Before I left the room, she caught my hand.

"Don't go." I could barely smile at her.

"I love you." I kissed her forehead before I left the room. My next stop was Dan's room.

"Hey, Dan." He looked up at me from his sprawled position on his bed. "I-I'm going to be leaving for a while." Dan stood up.

"Alli...What are you talking about?" He sounded a little freaked out.

"I made a deal with someone, and it involves me leaving for the summer. I'll be back after that, but Mom will be better and-" I stopped talking, but pulled Dan into a tight hug. Normally, he would squirm out of my grip, but right now, he latched on tightly to me.

35

"Just make sure you come back. We need you here." His voice was muffled as he spoke. I just nodded, not trusting my voice.

Dan followed me to the front door, his eyes widening when he recognize Joshua.

"I'll be back. I promise." Dan just nodded, still staring at Joshua.

"She'd better be safe." In a different situation, it would be amusing to watch a twelve-year-old boy speak like this to a twenty-something year old man. But it wasn't amusing today.

One more hug and I followed Joshua away from my home. We walked for a couple of blocks before we came to a small, dark red car. I recognized Carter sitting behind the steering wheel. Joshua held the door open for me, and I got in, refusing to look at him. He climbed into the backseat with me and shut the door behind him while Carter started up the engine.

We drove for about an hour, passing neighborhoods, the city limits, and, finally, small sections of forest. Eventually, we wound up on a winding cliffside road. One side was sheer rock, while the other side dropped off into the sea. Normally, it would be a beautiful sight, but I couldn't find any beauty in it at the time. The sea seemed as cold and dark as the night sky, and the cliffside loomed menacingly above me. A small hint of orange still lingered in the sky, but that was quickly fading. Hopefully, that wasn't a sign.

~*~

Brent was waiting outside when the car drove up. He was sitting at the edge of the cliff, leaning against a tree while one leg dangled off the edge. He could recognize the dark red car from miles away, and when the car came to a stop, he leaned forwards slightly, wondering who Joshua and Carter had found. He knew that they had been going back to the same girl several times in the past couple of days. Maybe they had finally gotten her to come.

He watched as Joshua got out of the back seat and held the door open for someone. A girl did indeed climb out of the car after him. He could tell, even from a distance, that she was very nervous and jumpy. He didn't blame her.

Brent rested his elbows on his knees, trying to get a better look at the girl's face. She didn't seem to be very tall and was pale and slender with short dark hair. She looked familiar...

He stood up and went inside. Best to get the first meeting over with as soon as possible. He hated them. It just reminded him of who he was. He paused briefly once inside to let his eyes adjust to the darkness. He then went down several steps, but stopped at the bottom in the darkest shadows, waiting for the girl to come into the room.

He could hear them coming. The girl's eyes were looking everywhere, as though waiting for something to jump out of the shadows. Allison. Oh yes. He remembered her.

Brent silently punched the wall next to him. What did God have against him?!

He quickly took several deep breaths and composed himself, putting on a blank face as the small group came to a stop next to the fire.

~*~

When the car began to slow down, I took more notice of what was going on around me. As I shifted in my seat, I winced when I put pressure on my left hand. It was still throbbing. There was absolutely no home or livable place in sight along the road, so I wondered why Carter was looking so closely at the cliff wall on the left side of the road.

The car came to a halt after Joshua pointed something out, which I obviously couldn't see. Joshua got out of the back seat and held the door open for me. I quietly got out of the car, panicking on the inside as thoughts of everything bad that could possibly happen in the next couple of moments flashed through my mind.

"What are we doing here?" Joshua could obviously hear the fear in my voice.

"Don't worry. Nothing's going to happen to you." Easy for them to say!

Carter turned off the car and got out to join us. He stood next to me, while Joshua ran a hand along the side of the cliff. Finally, he stopped.

"Found it." He looked over at us before disappearing.

"Holy crap!" I yelped, jumping back. "What was that?" Carter ignored me but only motioned me over to where Joshua had disappeared. When I followed, he suddenly gave me a shove that sent me directly into the cliffside. I let out a strangled yell when I didn't hit the stone. Instead, darkness swallowed me and I crashed into someone. They grabbed hold of me to stop me from falling over.

"Relax." It was Joshua. I realized that I could just see his outline from a fire that looked to be far away. It looked like we were in a stone corridor. Moments later, Carter suddenly appeared next to us and the two men led me down the hallway.

At the end of it, there was a large stone room with next to nothing in it, except for a large fire in the middle. The fire cast long, eerie shadows at random places on the walls and ceiling. There were two dark openings to the room, not counting the one from which we had just come. It looked like was another hallway, and the other was a flight of stairs.

We came to a halt next to the fire and they stepped back a little. I looked at them.

"Guys? Where I am?" This place was creepy. "Why did you bring me here?" They swore I would be safe, but I still wasn't so sure.

"Where you are and what you are here for isn't important to you, Allison." The soft but firm answer came from behind me, causing me to jerk and twist to see who the new person was. I almost screamed at the sight of the man now in front of me. He was very tall and tan and muscular. He had close cropped hair that looked almost brown, but I couldn't tell for sure. What scared me though was what covered him. He looked like he had been in a fight with a lion and lost. Deep scars covered his body. The thick twisted veins of white and sometimes red roped around his arms, legs, and face. One scar in particular ran directly across his face, from the side of his forehead, across his nose, and ending at the corner of his jawline. Another riveting scar branched out from that one and cut through his lips and chin. It looked as if his lips had healed for the most part, but what was around them cut deep like thin ditches.

I settled for a loud gasp and jerked backwards almost unconsciously. Of course, I managed to trip while doing so, and ended up falling towards the fire, arms reeling. Quick as lightning, the scarred man lunged towards me and caught my arm in a steel-like grip just before I hit the flames.

The heat was almost as painful as the grip the man had on me in order to keep me away from the flames, and I let out a wounded cry. With an impatient look on his face, the scarred man pulled me upright and let me go. He didn't look happy, so I tried to not make any noise. I put a hand over the spot where he had gripped me. As much as it had hurt, I guess *that* was better than getting burned severely.

The scarred man went over to one of the walls and took down an old fashion torch and lit it by the fire. He then went over to the opening in the wall that led to some stairs. I knew that this would be the perfect opportunity to run away, but then I remembered the whole reason that I was here. There was no way that I trusted these men, but they had fulfilled their end of the bargain...so far.

"Follow me." The scarred man was looking straight at me, so I hesitantly did what he said. He didn't look like someone who could be messed with, and I now had no choice. I looked back at Joshua and Carter, but they only stood there, not giving me any reason to obey or not. I followed the man holding the torch. The stairs sloped gently upwards and to the right, and without the torch, it would have been pitch black.

The stairs soon ended in what was soon revealed to be a hallway. As soon as the scarred man stepped into it, about five or six torches sprang to life, illuminating stone walls and stone floors. I let out a gasp. How had that happened? There were only a few doors, but there was a considerable amount of space between each one. The scarred man stopped at the first door on the right.

"You may go through this door to the library. That door," he pointed to the door directly across the hall. "you are not to use under any circumstance."

"Why?" I almost immediately regretted asking when the man stared at me hard.

"Because I say." I fell silent afterwards and he turned away and continued down the hall. He passed the next door on the left and went to the last one, which was where the hallway ended. He opened it and placed the torch into a metal holder inside.

The first thing I noticed about this room was that it had a large window, something that was missing in the rest of the dark, cave-like place. It

41

showed a view of the opaque ocean below. I stared out at the view for several moments, not moving from my position in the doorway until someone cleared his throat. I jumped and jerked my gaze towards the scarred man, who was standing next to a sink built into the stone wall, which looked very out of place in a room made of dull grey rock.

"Give me your hand." I looked down at my throbbing left hand and found that the bandages had started to come undone with blood seeping through the thin layers. I carefully gave him my hand, watching in silence as the man took off the bandage.

I winced at the sight of the blood crusted around the large gash. The man ran water over my palm and I watched as dried flakes of blood came off. In a couple of places, new blood came to the surface, only to be washed away.

After a moment, the man turned off the water and gave me a thin towel to dry off my hand. I held it carefully over the cut while he opened a cabinet and took out a small jar and some new bandages. He opened the jar and rubbed some sort of cream over the cut, before wrapping my hand up once more with the bandages.

While he did this, I took some time to study the scarred man in the firelight. It looked like he spent a lot of time in the sun, which made me wonder where he went in his spare time. Then again, I wasn't so sure I wanted to know. I couldn't imagine what had happened to him that would have caused the scars. In the dim lighting, they seemed to

42

all be a brilliant white. I dropped my gaze to my hand as he wrapped it. His own hands were large and enveloped mine. I looked back at his face only for him to look up as well and catch me staring at him. I blushed slightly in embarrassment and looked down. Again.

The man finished wrapping my hand and then let go. He was already outside of the door before he spoke. My hand tingled as the warmth of his hands left.

"Follow me." I didn't really want to, but did so anyway. The man had picked up the torch once more and was heading to the door that he had previously skipped before. He opened it to another flight of stairs, which he went up.

When I stepped out of the darkness of the stairway, I found myself in a small living room area. There was a giant floor length open window. There were wooden doors that could close on either side of it. I made a mental note not to fall off the edge.

There was a small, bench-like couch that was a gross green color against one of the stone walls and a small coffee table, but besides that, there was nothing. Nothing but grey and beige stone. In the corner, there was another shadowy doorway with a couple steps, but I could clearly see into the area. It was a bedroom. I started to silently panic about what might happen.

"This is where you will stay." I jerked impulsively at the sound of the scarred man's voice, glancing over at him nervously, but he made no

43

moves. He turned around and began to walk back to the stairs, leaving the area.

"I'm to stay here?" My voice surprised me, and I held my breath as the man pause for a moment before turning towards me slightly.

"Yes." He sounded as if he had had this conversation before. "Would you rather be locked in a closet or tied up?"

"No." I said quickly. He turned back to the stairs.

"Then I suggest you don't complain. Rest. When you hear the chiming in the morning, you will come down to the dining area. It's the first room; the one with the fire pit in it."

With that, he was gone. I let out the shaky breath I had been holding and looked around my new living space. I hesitantly walked up the few steps to the bedroom, half expecting someone to jump out and attack me, but there was nothing but the quiet, stone walls, a hard looking bed, and a nightstand. There was another large window about ten feet from the bed, and I walked over to it. Looking out, I finally realized that the room I was in was cut directly into the cliffside. I wondered how I hadn't figured that out before. The view was nothing less than breathless. It was truly magical! But at the moment, there was no way I could appreciate it at all.

My mind was racing a thousand miles a minute. I was in a cave turned home. In a cliffside. Mom was finally going to get better, and I wouldn't be there to see it. Had I done the right thing? After all, it was only for the summer...

A lot could happen in a summer.

Tears suddenly came. All of the emotions from the past day unlocked, and I collapsed against the side of the window. Silent tears ran down my face as I looked at the ocean. Why me?

~*~

Brent pulled the door shut behind Allison for the night and immediately dropped his blank mask. He quickly went through the door he had forbidden her to open and shut it behind him. He climbed several stairs until he reached the top and looked angrily around his own room. It was lit by four torches, since the main light source- a large floor length window- was currently blocked by a wooden door. The firelight suited his mood perfectly fine.

"Auggh!" Brent hit the wall in frustration, screaming his frustration. "I am so sick of this!" He could feel the scar tissue on his face pull as he shouted. It wasn't a pleasant sensation, but it didn't hurt. It was just a constant reminder.

He jerked away from the wall and flung open one of the several doors in his room. It led to a small dark room with a floor length mirror.

"Show me Allison!" He said harshly, closing the door behind him and sinking down to the floor directly opposite the mirror. For a moment, his own hideous reflection remained before it slowly morphed into the shape of Allison.

45

She was also on the ground. From what he could see, she was sitting at the window in her bedroom, leaning against the side. She was staring at the sea with eyes that weren't really seeing anything. She was absolutely still. No movement. One would almost think it was a portrait but for the small silvery trails of tears coursing down her face. Her eyes held the pain of hopelessness.

Brent turned his eyes away from the image. He was a fool hoping for what he knew could never happen. All he ever did was cause pain. And that's all he would ever do.

Chapter 3

A loud, clear chiming woke me, and I quickly opened my eyes. The first thing I saw was a stone wall. So it was true. It wasn't a dream. I shuddered as I slowly uncurled from my position on the floor. I sat there, not wanting to move more than needed and definitely not wanting to go downstairs to eat with those men.

The sunrise was just now coming to a close, so I sat and waited for the morning sky to turn completely blue. There was no way that I was going to eat with those men. It didn't matter that my stomach was growling. I had skipped meals before. They would just have to deal with it. I spent the duration of the day wandering around my new living area and my room, dozing off and on.

It wasn't until the third time that I heard the loud chiming that someone cleared their throat. I jumped at the sound, even though I had been expecting it. I looked over and saw Joshua standing at the base of the steps, obviously waiting for me. I took my time standing up and walking across the bedroom. When I reached the top of the stairs, Joshua stepped away, waiting for me to pass. I did so cautiously, but he did nothing but follow behind me. When I reached the dining area, I hesitated in the darkness of the stairway for a moment. There were four wooden chairs facing the fire. The scarred man and the Carter were already sitting down, holding plates of food.

Joshua went and sat down in the chair next to Carter, leaving the only remaining seat next to the scarred man. I carefully went over and found a plate of food on the chair. I picked it up and sat down, all the while keeping a wary eye on the men at all times.

For a while, an awkward silence reigned, before I tentatively broke it.

"What should I call you?" I didn't look at anyone in particular, but after a moment, the scarred man answered for everyone.

"You may call me Brent." I didn't believe this was his real name, but I hadn't been expecting it either.

"Okay." It is really strange trying to talk to your kidnappers when they don't have much expression. I wondered if this was normal. "What about you two?" I motioned at Joshua and Carter. "You did give me your real names, right?" Carter looked like he was going to tell me some really complicated name, but Joshua gave him a look.

"Yes, those are our names." He addressed me while Carter scowled at his food.

I nodded, waiting for one of them to continue, but silence reigned once more. I had to mentally fortify myself in order to continue my questioning.

"I need proof that you are upholding your end of the bargain. How do I know that my mom is better?"

The three men look at each other in silent conversation before Joshua addresses me.

"You can send letters to each other. The next time either Carter or I go into town, we can give your mom a letter and wait for a reply."

I took a deep breathe. That would work.

"Okay." If I didn't get a response, then I would know that I had better get out of this place sooner, rather than later.

After this exchange, I found out very quickly that I was quite hungry, and my plate was soon empty. I could have probably eaten more, but there wasn't anything around. In the end, I just set my plate down on the ground. Eventually, I grew tired of waiting for...well, nothing, so I stood up and was almost to the stairway when the scarred man, Brent, stopped me.

"Do you have a watch?" If not for the situation I was in, I probably would have laughed at how random the question seemed.

"No." I said slowly, looking back. Brent was quiet for a moment.

"At 9 o'clock PM, the lights will all go out. Be sure to be in your room before that time. Breakfast is served at 7:30 AM." He turned back to the fire, and I stared at his back for a moment longer before going up the stairs.

49

I thought about Brent's actions. So far he hadn't made any move to harm me at all. Strange. In fact, he seemed to care if I was hurt. I might have been touched if not for the fact that he was blackmailing me for some reason unknown.

I stopped halfway up the stairs, just able to make out bits of conversation floating up the stairs from behind me. I heard my name mentioned once. I bit my lip, trying to decide whether it was worth the risk of going back down there in order to hear what they were saying. In the end, I found myself not caring enough. As the only girl in this place, of course they were going to talk about me. Just that thought was disturbing enough to prompt me to head to the library for some solace.

To get to the library I didn't need to climb up any steps, but climb down. Steps spiraled downward, and I hurried to get to the bottom, still worried about being seen. But, as soon as I reached the bottom I forgot about the men above, and I literally froze.

There were books everywhere. The room was tall, long, and brimming with ornately carved bookshelves. None of the shelves seemed to be made of the same wood, and in the firelight it looked as though the shadows were the cause for the different colors of the wood grains. There were a few large, plush chairs in the corner directly opposite from the entrance. Trying to absorb all of the elaborate details, I referred back to my previous thought. There were books everywhere! Books were on the shelves, in waist high piles on the ground, and even on top of the chairs. It was almost a dangerous hazard to move around in that room, but I loved it. It was like entering a dream. So far, the books seemed to be the only truly normal thing around here. Although, there were so many that it really wasn't normal at all.

I went up to the nearest bookshelf and ran the tips of my fingers along the spines of the books. To my disappointment, they all seemed to be histories of war. I kept reading the titles though, hoping to come across a more interesting book, but I quickly got tired of reading titles. I guess the real problem was that I was physically exhausted. Meandering around the place, I quickly decided that of all of the rooms in this cave dwelling, I liked this one the most.

~*~

"Do you have a watch?" Brent knew it was stupid to be kind, especially since she would run away at the first chance.

"No." She answered...Which was a plus! At least she was speaking to him.

"At 9 o'clock PM, the lights will all go out. Be sure to be in your room before that time. Breakfast is served at 7:30 AM." He turned away from her. A moment later, he could hear her moving up the stairs. He waited until her footsteps faded before he slumped in his chair and groaned. It just had to be her.

"Hey," Joshua brought up the topic. "You knew her name. Did you know her?" Brent almost laughed. It was as though Joshua had read his mind.

51

"Oh, did I ever…" Joshua and Carter both waited for Brent to continue as he stared into the fire. "She went to my school with me."

"Does that mean it will be easier or harder?"

"It's already hard. But I have a feeling that it will get worse. We didn't exactly get along."

"Well, was she-" Brent cut Carter off.

"No, there was never anything between us. If anything, she hated me with all she could. I even remember her spitting at me once." Carter stood up as Brent fell into a brooding silence.

"Hey," He said. "We'll figure this out. We still have the summer."

Brent didn't respond. The summer suddenly seemed very short.

~*~

At last, I pulled myself away from the library and made my way back to my room.

When I was about halfway down the hallway, everything suddenly went dark. I let out a gasp, and almost had a heart attack when I heard something move in the darkness. It was a struggle to keep from screaming. A door suddenly opened in the darkness and moonlight flooded the hallway. I could just make out the figure of Brent holding the door to the medical room open, standing mostly in the shadows. I calmed my breathing and found my way to the door to my room. I placed my hand on the knob, before turning back to thank Brent, but no one was there. I quickly shut the door and ran up the stairs to the living room area.

Sitting on the ledge of the window, I watched the city skyline in the distance. This place was way too strange. The more I thought about it, the more it became harder to explain. Why on earth would these men want me here? The only reasonable explanations creeped me out. After thinking a little longer, I made up my mind. I rummaged around the room, eventually coming up with some paper and a pen. I began to write a letter to Mom. In the morning, I would pass it off to Joshua and Carter, and if I didn't get a response that night, I would run.

~*~

The lights went out just before Brent could close his bedroom door. A loud gasp stopped him from shutting it all the way. Of course Allison wasn't in her room. He opened the door and stepped into the hallway. He could just make out her frozen figure, only about ten feet from her door. He quickly passed her and opened the door to the medical room, flooding the hall with moonlight. Brent kept to the shadows as best he could when he saw the terrified look on her face and hoped that she wouldn't stare. He waited until her back was turned before he escaped to his own room and shut the door.

A few minutes later, he was watching through the mirror as Allison sat at the window again, looking at the sea. Only this time she looked angry and determined. He had seen that look before. He would have to make sure that someone was always keeping watch in the dining area. She was going to run.

~*~

The next day, I waited anxiously for dinner time to come around, but when it did, Joshua just told me that they hadn't been able to deliver the letter yet. I didn't believe them.

I got ready to run, but the following day, no matter when I went into the dining area, there was always someone there.

Over the next several days, I began to skip more and more meals, barely coming out of my room, if I could help it. Almost a week passed this way, and I could tell from the way the men were looking at me, they weren't too thrilled with it. I needed to get out of here. I hadn't ever gotten the letter from Mom, and, until I did, there was no reason to stay.

Finally though, the opportunity presented itself. I was starving, so I decided to go to lunch. When I walked into the dining area, no one was there. I jumped at the chance, and ran to the entrance hallway. I got about a third the way down the passage before I heard Brent's voice call out for me to stop. I kept running. By the time I was halfway down the hallway, Brent had caught up with me. He caught my arm and held it. I realized later on that I could have easily pulled away, but my mind was working on overload and my breath was already short. I could feel myself hyperventilating, and I almost collapsed trying to sit down. My heart raced.

I could faintly hear Brent yelling out to Joshua and Carter, but most of my attention was focused on trying to breathe normally. My escape turned out to be a disaster.

~*~

So she had tried to run.

Brent had caught up to her before she had gotten away, but he hadn't expected her to begin to hyperventilate when he grabbed her arm. He didn't really know what he had been thinking. He guessed that it must have been the small part of him that just wanted to have the curse end, no matter who it was who ended it. He just wanted to be normal again.

He yelled out for Joshua and Carter when Allison had collapsed on the ground. As soon as they got to where he was with Allison, he left.

He didn't really want to know the reason for her panic attack; he already had a pretty good idea. He soon found himself on the edge of the cliff outside, sitting under one of the trees in the shade.

"I hate my life." He muttered to himself.

"Hate it all you want. Just never take it." Brent looked up sharply to see her. It was the woman. The enchantress.

"I won't." His voice was void of emotion. "But you already knew that. It's been almost two years since you were last here. Why show up now? What do you want?" He suddenly felt exhausted as he turned back to the vast sea. The woman sat down with him. He didn't move.

"I want to know if you are going to try again."

"No."

"No, as in you won't tell me, or no, as in-"

"No, as in: I give up." He turned to her at last. "I give up. You win. I hope you're happy." She looked disappointed in him. "Besides, this summer is the last. Magic can only keep that flower alive for so long when there is little for it to live on."

"I see."

"No. You don't." He looked at the sea again. "You don't really."

"Yes. I do. I created the spell, remember? The magic around this place will recognize the One before anyone else. Even me." She caught Brent's eye and held it. "And from what I can sense in the magic, she has already been here. The magic is already changing."

"Well that's helpful." Brent replied sarcastically. "You do realize how many girls have come and gone since the last time you've been here?" The enchantress smiled knowingly.

"Yes, three girls, including her. Do not worry. Whoever it is-is still here."

"Allison?" Brent couldn't believe his ears. The same girl who was currently inside recovering from a panic attack that he caused because he had touched her arm. He seriously doubted it was her. "She's not even here willingly." He stated.

"Of course she is. She came because her family needed help. Eventually, she will stay for a different reason." Brent gave a harsh laugh.

"Eventually? Do you even hear yourself?! Why am I listening to you? You're the reason I'm in this mess! I have one summer left! The only possible way someone might fall in love me by the end of this summer is if they were blind!"

"True love isn't about looks."

Brent snorted.

"If everyone who sees me runs away screaming, 'Monster!' or 'Freak!', don't you think that this philosophy might not work?"

"No, I don't."

Brent just shook his head. After a small silence she stood up. "I wish you the best of luck, Mark."

"Brent. My name is Brent."

"Very well, Brent." With that she left him alone.

~*~

By the time that Brent came back inside from his temporary mental breakdown, Carter was waiting for him.

"About time you stopped moping."

Brent glared at him.

"Oh, well that's so kind of you to ask. Alli is doing fine." Carter continued his conversation single-handedly. "She only experienced a panic attack and ended up passing out before her heart rate returned to normal." Brent could see where Carter was taking this.

"Before you continue, I left because I caused the panic attack." Carter's eyebrows rose.

"And why would you cause something like that?"

"Why do you think?" Brent scoffed. A moment later, he took a deep breath to calm himself. "How is she?" Thankfully, Carter didn't comment on his first reply, but only led him back down to the dining room.

Joshua was down there, sitting next to Allison, who was propped up against one of the walls, unconscious. He looked up at them when they walked in, but didn't say anything.

"How long has she been unconscious?"

"About ten minutes now."

"Why is she still down here?" Joshua laughed at Brent's question and stood up.

"That, muscle man, it what you are here for." Brent rolled his eyes, but picked Allison up anyway. He carried her up to the medical room and set her down on the table.

"Well." Carter clapped his hands together as Brent set her down. "Now that she's here, I'm off. Have fun." He clapped Brent's shoulder as he left the room, and Joshua glanced at Brent.

"You would think, by now, that he would realize that there are only so many places he can go in this place." Brent couldn't help but chuckle at the statement. "But," Joshua continued. "he does have a point. So long." He clapped Brent on the shoulder as well and left him to watch after Allison. He scowled. Of course they had set him up.

He looked at Allison. Alli. That's what Joshua and Carter had been calling her. Was that what she went by now? Well, it made sense. The name fit her better than Allison. Alli.

While he waited for her to wake up, he went ahead and changed the bandage around her hand. The cut was healing slowly, which made sense, considering how deep it was. It would definitely leave a scar across her palm. He wondered what had caused it.

Brent spent the next several minutes staring out of the window at the sea. When he heard some noise behind him, he turned and saw that Alli was shifting in her sleep. Her face had twisted into a frown. He really hoped she wasn't going to wake up, only to have another panic attack.

Suddenly, she jerked up, screaming. She sounded as though she had lost most of her voice and couldn't get all of her breath out of her lungs. All in all, it freaked Brent out.

He put a hand against her back. This action brought back to his mind the time that he had been so sick that he had stayed up all night, throwing up. His mom had been by his side the whole time.

To be honest, Brent was startled when a second later Alli leaned into his touch, now sobbing as though her heart was broken. He did what any guy would do. He held her in his arms until her tears came to a stop, and she pulled away. He guessed the only downside to this was that she didn't know it was him because she still hadn't opened her eyes.

Chapter 4

I woke up screaming.

I jerked into a sitting position, screaming and crying at the same time. I heard a noise somewhere in my subconsciousness, but it didn't truly register. There was a warmth on my back, and I leaned into it, desperate for comfort. Slowly my tears came to a halt, and I found myself more able to control my breathing.

I found myself pressed against someone's chest, and as soon as I realized this, I immediately pulled away and curled in on myself. I opened my eyes to find myself staring at a cold stone wall and a horribly scarred face. Instead of shrieking, as I might normally do, I just closed my eyes again, a small whimper escaping through my lips. A few moments passed in silence before I spoke softly.

"What happened?" I looked pleadingly at Brent, who was looking at me with what seemed to be concern.

"I don't know." He spoke softly. "From what I saw and what Carter told me, you had a panic attack and passed out." I didn't reply to this, but only curled in on myself more. "Are you in pain?" I have to admit: I wouldn't think that he would care about something like that. I thought for a moment before I decided that the raging headache tearing through my skull hurt enough to mention.

"A headache." Brent got up and went over to a beautiful wooden cabinet. He opened it and took out a small jar, different from the one he used before on my cut. There seemed to be a type of lotion in it, which he rubbed onto my forehead. I drew back at first, but I didn't stop him. The lotion felt cool against my skin and almost immediately I felt my headache start to go away.

"What is that?" I felt slightly embarrassed at how curious I sounded, but felt reassured when Brent didn't look angry.

"It's a lotion, so to speak, to cure headaches." I remained silent, too tired to figure out why a lotion that cured headaches made no sense in my mind. "I also changed the bandage around your hand, so you don't worry about that later."

I slowly uncurled my body from its position and attempted to sit up. The pain in my head had faded into a dull throb that I could now stand. I saw that he had indeed changed the bandage around my hand. I hesitated to speak again, but he hadn't been angry before, so I risked it.

"Are you angry?" My voice was so quiet that I was surprised that he heard me at all. For the longest time, Brent didn't say anything, but then he spoke quietly.

"No." We both refused to look at the other.

"Where do the medicines, salves, and lotions come from?" Brent looked almost relieved that I hadn't remained quiet. Almost. His face was a blank wall that very few emotions ever slipped through.

"The room provides you with what you need." He seemed to be suggesting that it was by magic that this happened, but I wrote it off as a side effect of the panic attack.

"How do you know what to do?"

"Instructions appear on the inside of the cabinet." He pointed to the same wooden cabinet that the lotion had come from.

"Oh..." There must be a book in there with the instructions written down for different situations. What else was there for me to say? "Thank you." I said softly. The dull look in his eyes slipped, and I saw that Brent was surprised.

"Y-You're welcome." He tried to cover the slip up, and I pretended to not notice. It was obvious that he hadn't been thanked before, or at least in a very long time.

~*~

By the time I found myself back in my 'room' it was nearing dark. I sighed at the sight of the hard stone wall and floor. I doubted that I would ever be able to make an attempt to escape again. I would just have to keep reminding myself why I was here in the first place.

I went over everything in the bedroom section for what seemed to be the thousandth time. There was a double bed made of delicately carved white wood, which was nice. I had never owned

63

anything other than a twin bed. Next to the bed was a small wooden nightstand made of a wood so light, it looked white, and above that was a pale wooden torch connected to the wall. There was also a door made up of the same wood as everything else, which led to a rather large bathroom. In the bathroom, things looked less medieval. There was a shower and sink, both of which had running water, although they were made of stone. At least there was a mirror. Thank the Lord for small miracles.

I took a long shower, wondering what part of this day had been a dream and what hadn't. This question kept me awake long after the shower and late into the night. Everything here seemed to be only semi-normal, and there were several things that didn't add up completely in a logical way.

A couple of minutes passed in peace before someone knocked on my door. I felt my heartrate speed up in spite of myself as I walked to the door. I opened it to find Joshua holding something in his hands. He passed it to me. It was a letter.

"Sorry it took so long to get this to you." Joshua shifted in place.

"Thank you." I felt bubble of happiness rise inside of me.

As soon as I closed the door, I tore the envelope open with shaking hands and let out a sigh of relief at the sight of Mom's handwriting covering several pieces of paper. I settled onto my bed to read it all.

By the end, I was amazed. In my heart, I never believed that the men would uphold their end of the bargain, but they had. The house was secure for the next several months, and Mom's energy had returned almost to normal. It was a blessing, and yet a curse. I didn't want to stay here, but now I had to. For once, everything at home was good, but I wasn't there to enjoy it. It was a bittersweet sorrow.

~*~

Brent spent that night outside. He felt as though there was something wrong with the fact that Allison-Alli was still here.

If the enchantress was right and she was the one...

Brent punched a tree. He stared at the split skin on his knuckles with a morbid fascination until the pain registered in his mind. He quickly wiped away the blood on his shirt. Even if Alli could somehow grow to love him, when she found out that he was the boy who had treated her like dirt in the past, she would most definitely hate him. He knew that it could never happen. Who, in their right mind, could ever love someone as scarred as him, someone cursed because of their pride, someone they hated? If she knew the full truth, she would see him as he really was: a beast.

~*~

I finally woke up the next day to beautiful sunlight and someone banging unhappily on the door to my bedroom. I stumbled out of the hard bed, still in yesterday's clothes, and yanked open the door to a fist about to slam into my face. I jerked back quickly, not wanting to be hit for any reason, almost tumbling to the floor. The first thought I had was of the two men who had come knocking at my door the same night Joshua and Carter had struck the deal with me. Many other unpleasant memories also arose at the sight from the past several school years, causing me to freeze up.

The person behind the fist turned out to be Joshua. He quickly pulled back his balled hand when he saw that he was about to hit me.

"Sorry, but you weren't answering." I just stared at him, but before I could gather myself up enough to ask anything, he kept talking. "Look. I know that you've been through a lot, but you have got to start coming to meals. Lunch was just served" When I didn't speak, he just spun around and left. When I was sure that he was gone, I felt like pinching myself. Why didn't I speak when I had the chance?

I have to admit: It did cross my mind to just go on ahead and skip lunch, but fear won out, so I settled for arriving late instead. In the hallway I ran into Brent who, judging by the annoyed look on his face, was just about to come and get me. I looked down and moved past him silently, forcing him to turn around and follow me to the cavernous dining area.

Lunch was awkward, especially after that, so I settled for eating in silence. I kept my eyes trained on my plate as much as possible, even though I could feel Brent's eyes burning a hole through my head. I felt so nervous that when I tried to take a sip of my water, I choked as it went down the wrong pipe. I started coughing so hard that

Brent had to reach over and thump my back in order to get me to stop. I nodded my thanks to him as I put down my plate. I massaged my eyes before standing up to leave. There was no way that I would be able to eat anything more today, especially when he was watching me so closely. Who would want a guy watching you eat?

I made my way to my room and shut the door behind me. Even here in the safety on the room, I felt as though Brent was watching my every move. I moved to the bedroom portion of my new living space and once more categorized all of the objects in the room. The bed. The nightstand. The torch. The wardrobe...Which I had never seen before in my entire life.

I did a double look, but the wardrobe was still there. I walked over slowly and ran my fingers over the deeply stained wood. It was the only wooden object that wasn't built out of pale wood. Tiny carved flowers were scattered in a delicate pattern that seemed to look like they were being carried by the wind when I stood back. It was gorgeous!

I carefully opened it and found to my amazement that it was full of clothes. As I looked again, I recognized the majority of them as the clothes from my own closet! I rubbed my eyes. This made no sense. I had been washing the couple of shirts and shorts that I had brought with me in the sink and hanging them up to dry. Well, now I had my whole closet of clothes. I would definitely need to speak to someone about this. Those men had better not have gone back to my house to get these.

I grabbed a new outfit from the wardrobe and changed. I dumped the old ones in a corner, determined to ask someone what to do with them. Maybe I should just go ahead and keep washing them myself in the bathroom? It would be nice if I didn't need to do that. I'd have to figure that out later. Right now I was just glad to have new clothes. It was kind of nice knowing that something from my real home was here.

I started to walk out of the bedroom, when I remembered something. I ran back to the wardrobe and began to search for a certain pair of pants. Eventually, I successfully found what I was looking for. Inside one of the back pockets was a picture that had been taken of my family when we had gone skiing in Colorado. It was the only time we had ever gone together, and no matter how hard I had tried, I was a terrible skier. The picture was taken at the top of one of the mountains at sunrise. Dan and I were sandwiched between mom and dad. All of us had large goofy grins on our face, but no one cared. It was one of my favorite memories of being with my family.

But that was before Mom had gotten sick, before Dad had begun to pull away, and before our financial problems.

The memory of that happy time brought tears to my eyes. I quickly sat down at the window and squeezed my eyes shut. Somehow, everything had to be fine. I could recall reading a quote somewhere that read: *Everything will be okay in the end. If it's not okay, it's not the end.*

I wished with all my heart that that quote was true. I needed it to be true, now more than ever.

Before I knew it, my eyes had shut and I was taken away to a place where my desperate wishes could come to life.

~*~

That night I came to dinner on time. You would think that after several days had passed that it might become easier to talk to the men who were keeping you locked away in a cliff home, but I wasn't finding this to be the case. Well, I wanted some answers, and it was either now or never. I waited until everyone was about halfway done eating before I began questioning.

"When did you start living here?" I guess I should have started with a different question. At my words, everyone stopped eating and turned to look at me. I couldn't tell if they were annoyed or surprise that I had attempted to make a conversation. I flushed and nervously looked down at my lap where my plate was before looking back up. "Well?" Finally though, Brent answered.

"About two years ago." He was staring hard at me, and it made me feel a bit uncomfortable.

"Why here?" It was a honest question.

"Because." Brent's tone was hard and clipped. I bit my lip, wondering if I should continue.

"But-" Brent cut me off.

"You know in all the time I'd-" He cut himself off this time and quickly stood up. I stood up as well, startled by his sudden movement. He turned and quickly left the room, leaving a deathly silence in his wake. I looked cautiously at Joshua and Carter, but they said nothing. Joshua was staring into the fire while Carter was going in between looking at the doorway Brent had disappeared through and me. I bit my lip again. Dinner was definitely over.

I had already eaten my fill, so I left the dining area and made my way up to my room. At the end of the hallway, I saw Brent in the medical room, leaning against the window in there, looking at the sea.

I tried to get through my door quietly, but it was to no avail. Almost the moment I touched it, a loud screech echoed in the air, causing me to cringe. Brent hardly moved. He looked behind him and must have seen me, but he didn't acknowledge me. He brushed past me and went to the forbidden room. It must have been his bedroom.

~*~

"You know in all the time I've-" Brent cut himself off when he realized what he was saying. He had almost given himself away! He had to get out of here. He quickly stood up and exited the room, only vaguely realizing that Alli had stood up with him.

He climbed the stairs and instead of going to his room or outside to vent out his anger, he found himself in the medical room. He went over to the window sill and leaned against it, letting the wind brush against his face.

What had he been thinking? Letting his anger get away from him! He hadn't slipped up around anyone like that in at least a year, so why on earth would he start now?

Brent had no idea.

A loud screech of hinges echoed in the hallway. He just closed his eyes. Alli. She must be trying to slip past him without disturbing him. She didn't seem to realize that if you just opened the door normally, it wouldn't make any noise at all.

He let out a small sigh and turned around to face the frozen form of Alli, who looked sorry that she had disturbed him. Yeah, right. He walked straight past her and went into his own room.

Once again, he found himself in front of the mirror. He had been coming to it more often now that she was here, but he would never admit that to anyone, especially himself.

"Show me Alli." He spoke in a tired voice as he leaned against the wall. The mirror revealed Allison just at the moment she caught her foot on a small step and fell. Brent rolled his eyes a little. Leave it to her to fall down. She caught herself just in time, but pain still registered on her face.

He watched as she discovered that her fall had been hard enough to reopen sections of her gash. The bandage around her palm now had growing dots of blood on them. She stood back up, holding her hand to her chest, and made her way back down to the medical room.

Brent could honestly say that he had never seen someone as accident prone as she was, except perhaps for himself. As she moved around the small room, he realized that she was having trouble. She was able to wash off the blood, dry her palm, and apply the salve just fine, but when it came to wrapping the new bandage around her palm, she wasn't making much progress. He rolled his eyes. He had done this to himself before. It wasn't that hard. He then realized that her face had grown pale. Maybe she hated the sight of blood? That might explain it.

Brent sighed, as he had been doing a lot lately. He'd better go down and help her. He severed the connection to the mirror and soon found himself standing at the door to the medical room. Alli was holding her hand under running water. She had her head resting against the table and her eyes closed. She was taking slow deep breaths. She must really hate the sight of blood. Brent almost felt sorry for her. Almost.

He allowed himself a small smile in amusement before getting rid of any expression on his face. Here goes nothing.

~*~

As I went into my own bedroom, I realized that I had never gotten to ask him about the wardrobe's appearance. Too late to do that now. I suddenly caught my foot on a step and fell forward. I managed to catch myself, but a sharp pain from the palm of my left hand caused me to jerk and hiss in pain. Oh great. Judging from the small bit of blood that was soaking through the bandage and the pain, the cut must have reopened a little. I thought that it would have healed by now, but apparently not. It must have been deeper than I originally thought.

I carefully sat up, holding my hand to my chest, and made my way to the medical room, thankful that Brent wasn't still there. I opened the wooden cabinet that Brent had previously pointed out to me and found a small glass jar filled with the blue tinted salve and some clean bandages. I took these off the shelf and brought them to the table in the middle of the room and stared at them for a moment, unsure of what to do. It was then that I remembered that Brent said that the instructions were on the inside of the cabinet door. I hadn't seen any sign of a medical book, but I went back over and looked at the cabinet door, just in case. Sure enough, there instructions were, written on the door. I felt a little stupid for needing them. I should know by now what to do. I had only watched Brent do it for me for the past couple of weeks. I guess that my attention span is pretty low. I read them over twice before doing what they said.

Taking the bandage off was easy, that is until I saw the blood underneath. I had to close my eyes and count to three before I could focus straight again. I quickly turned on the water in the sink and washed the blood off as best I could. To be honest, it didn't look like the cut was much better than before. It had reopened in two places. I looked around for something to dry my palm off with and saw some paper towels next to the sink that I could have sworn weren't there a moment before.

The next thing I had to do was apply the salve. It seemed as though this should have been easy, but for some reason, wherever I applied it only stung worse. The spots that had reopened turned the salve a dark red, which always creeped me out.

Then came the bandages. By this time, my hands were shaking so badly that it was way more difficult than it should have been. There was pain. There was blood. And I was tired. Eventually, I just gave up and washed the salve off. At last, the sharp pain went away, leaving behind a dull throb. I kept my hand under the water, not moving.

I didn't hear anyone enter the room, so when someone cleared his throat, I jumped, jerking my head up sharply. It was Brent. He was looking at me like he was trying to keep his emotions in check.

"You look like you could use some help." I nodded, surprised at his offer. How had he known that I was here? I quickly dried my palm off. He then took my hand in his and spread the salve over the cut himself. That was strange. My palm didn't sting when he did it. Once that was done, he proceeded to wrap it up. I stared at my hand in his. While his was large and calloused, mine was small and pale. There were several raised scars that traveled over the back of his hands and fingers. They looked like tiny ropes, although there were a couple that resembled ditches. They shone an eerie silver in the moonlight.

Brent soon finished and put the jar away. He left the used bandages in a corner on the counter. I followed him out of the medical room and was about to go to my room when he stopped me.

"If you change the bandage once a day for about a week longer, your hand should be healed by then. I'll meet you here after lunch each day to help like usual." I was grateful that he said that last bit. I don't think I could do it on my own, although I did wonder how he knew how long it would take.

"Okay."

"You will most likely have a scar, you know." I wasn't worried about that, especially now after I had seen what Brent lived with on a daily basis. I just then realized the most likely reason that he knew how long it would take was that he had had to do what I was doing in the past.

"Okay." I paused. "Thanks for the help. I needed it." I just noticed in the dim light how tense Brent got at that comment, but the tension was gone just as fast as it came. I could tell he wasn't used to being thanked often for whatever it was that he did. Finally, he just nodded in reply, and I left.

I sat up in the hard bed for a long time afterwards looking at the twinkling night sky outside. Why was I here? What could they possibly want with me? The question was driving me crazy.

Chapter 5

The next morning, sometime before breakfast, I found myself strangely awake and desperately bored in my room. At last, I could stand it no longer and made my way to the library. I kept my hopes up, just in case I could find an interesting book somewhere. After about five minutes, I found myself staring at the same couple of books over and over, so I decided to forgo my mission and head to the dining area. Now that I thought of it, I had never been in here except for meal times. The fire was still cheerfully burning as big as ever. I suddenly wondered where the wood for it came from. I had never seen any before. Strange.

The chairs that we would eat in were also out of sight. The room was basically empty. Well, how boring is that? I turned to leave and wander back to my room until breakfast, but Brent suddenly came in. He looked surprised to see me just standing there. To be honest, the firelight made him seem even more scary and intimidating. I was a little freaked out by the effect the light seemed to have on his eyes as well. They seemed to be glowing. It was creepy.

When he saw me, he stopped in his tracks, but before he could interrogate me, a question suddenly popped into my head.

"Umm...Do you have any paint?" I think I surprised him, because his normal scowl deepened.

"Why?"

"I need something to do." I surprised myself. Where the heck had that question come from? "Maybe some scenery, or..." I mused to myself, momentarily forgetting where I was. I snapped back to present day. "It would give me something to do." If Brent acted normal, he would probably be shaking his head in disbelief, but, of course, he wasn't normal, so he just raised an eyebrow.

"I'll see what I can find."

"Yes!" I reacted without thinking. "Thank you!" At the last minute, I blushed realizing that I sounded weird and a little hyper. Part of me wanted to crawl into a hole and die of embarrassment. The other part of me was trying to figure out what to paint.

A moment later, Carter stumbled into the room with a bleary look in his eyes that spoke of a need for caffeine. He scowled at the fire as though it was the fire's fault that he was tired.

"Your turn to go to the city for a supply run."

Carter looked up at Brent's words in dismay. "Why? Get Josh to do it." I assumed he was talking about Joshua.

"Whatever it is, I'm pretty sure I don't want to do it." I gave a small smile when I heard Joshua chime in to the conversation.

"To bad. You're doing it."

"You do it." Joshua frowned.

"No, you-"

"I was wondering if I could get some art supplies." I chimed in, cutting Carter off mid-argument. "To paint."

Both men looked at me before glaring at each other.

"I'll go." Carter grumbled, while Joshua stood smugly with his arms crossed. Carter turned to me. "What do you want?" I hesitated.

"Will you remember?"

"No." I felt like rolling my eyes, but thought better of it.

"Stay here. I'll grab some paper and make a list." I quickly left the room and grabbed paper. Just as I finished making the list, the breakfast bell rang. I grabbed the list and darted back down to the fire where the food was already laid out along with the chairs. I gave the list to Carter before sitting down, and he stuffed it in his pocket.

"Just out of curiosity," I hesitated when everyone paused and looked at me expectantly. "Umm. What do you and Joshua do in the city?" I wondered if this was one of the 'Off Limits' questions.

"We... How do describe what we do?" Carter turned to Joshua for help, and Joshua rolled his eyes.

"We're sort of like handymen. We do odd-end jobs that help people out of tough situations." I wondered if trapping girls in impossible situations

79

was considered 'helping'. I didn't say anything, only nodding to show I heard him.

Joshua left breakfast early, disappearing out the front entrance, and I soon abandoned my plate for the library to wait for Carter's return.

I held out for several hours, but when the lunch bell didn't signal fast enough, I made my way back down to the dining area to wait. The chairs were gone again, so I sat on the ground as close to the fire as I could without being uncomfortably warm. The room was cool enough to where the presence of the fire was welcoming. I hugged one of my knees, content just to watch the fire dance for now.

Someone cleared their throat behind me, and I jerked into an almost standing position. It was just Brent. I felt the need to explain myself to him, but I didn't know what I would say. I had already used up my backup excuse.

"Did you need anything?" Brent came to stand by the fire with me, and I held my breath, willing myself not to move away.

"No. I was just waiting for Carter to get back." I found I couldn't hold Brent's gaze, so I just looked at the fire.

Just then, the chimes signaled that it was time for lunch. The noise was much louder in here and seemed to be coming from the fire itself. I almost passed out when I saw what happened next. The wooden chairs that we have sat in for the past however many days just appeared out of thin air! I quickly backed up, finding myself pressed against the wall. Then, the plate of food came out of the fire and floated to each of the chairs! And that is when it happened. I passed out.

~*~

The first thought that came to Brent's mind when he entered the dining room was that Alli was trying to run away again. It wasn't quite lunch time yet, and that seemed like the obvious explanation. That explanation made him angry as well as slightly disappointed. She wouldn't even give him a chance? Then again, he had already told himself that he wouldn't let her.

He thought back to the moment that morning when she had been in here and asked for art supplies. It was as though she wanted to catch him off guard. Well, she had succeeded. The request was not at all what he had been expecting.

She was definitely the first girl to ever complain of boredom in this God forsaken place. She had a whole library at her disposal! He wanted to laugh at the absurdity of it. He had reluctantly agreed to try to find something for her, and her reaction had made it all worth it. Brent honestly had had to fight a smile off at the way she had thanked him. He had almost laughed outright when she suddenly froze and began blushing furiously as she realized what she had done.

The conversation that followed about whether or not Carter would go into town gave his a small hope that there was a chance for less awkward conversation. Alli still seemed insecure, but it was a start, right?

81

Brent forced his mind back to the present. Alli was just sitting on the floor next to the fire, watching it. He cleared his throat to alert her to his presence, and immediately regretted it. She was on her feet in no time, looking like a deer caught in the headlights of a car. Skepticism was evident in her eyes, especially as he moved closer.

"Did you need anything?" Was there anything he could say to make her less afraid?

"No. I was just waiting for Carter to get back." She bit her lower lip as though she had said too much, and Brent held back a sigh.

The loud lunch bell sounded from the fire. Brent realized that this would be Alli's first time to see this. She startled at the noise and watched the fire with rapt amazement. Everything happened as it normally would, but Brent kept a close eye on Alli. He knew this process wouldn't be normal to her. She looked completely shocked at the sight of how every meal arrived. Her face looked white as a sheet as she took slow, deliberate steps backwards, pressing herself against the wall. Then, she went limp. Her body completely collapsed in on itself as Brent quickly jumped forward and stopped her from a painful meeting with the floor.

Joshua and Carter managed to walk into the room right at that moment. Carter was holding several different art supplies.

"She passed out." Brent spoke before they could make any presuppositions as to why he was holding Alli in his arms. When they didn't respond, he glared at them irritated. "Well, are you going to help?"

Carter set down the stuff in his arms and helped him set her up against the stone wall, while Joshua knelt down next to them.

"What happened?" Joshua asked.

"She saw the food."

Carter snorted in laughter. "She passed out at the sight of food?"

Brent rolled his eyes. "No. She saw how it got here."

Carter grinned at the previous thought, and Brent also began to smile, when a soft moan came from Alli. The playfulness was gone as everyone looked at her as she opened her eyes.

~*~

I woke up to find myself looking into the concerned faces of Brent, Joshua, and Carter. All three were crouching down on the floor next to me. I was propped up against the wall with a small headache.

"Please tell me that I'm in a dream and not hallucinating." I whispered. If they told me that whatever it was I saw actually happened, then I might just pass out again.

"You aren't in a dream and you're not hallucinating." Carter spoke this in an overly cheerful voice. Well, I can happily say that I didn't pass out again, but I did glare at Carter.

I felt dazed and very out of it, but I tried to stand anyway. Brent helped me up. Nothing began to tilt, so I went ahead and made my way to my usual seat. I ate in silence and at a much slower pace than usual. Eventually, I couldn't eat anymore. I didn't acknowledge anyone when I left. I was stuck in my own thought process.

I managed to get all of the way up to my living area when I remembered that I needed to change the bandage around my hand. I slowly made my way to the medical room and found that Brent was waiting for me. Thankfully, he didn't try to make a conversation with me as he helped me. As soon as he finished tying off the bandage, I left to go to my room. Brent's voice made me pause at the doorway.

"Just so you know, this place is full of small magic like that." I stared at him for a moment before leaving without saying a word. Everyone here must be crazy, including me.

When I walked into my room, I stopped short at the sound of a knock from my door.

I backtracked and opened the door to find Carter standing there, holding a plastic bag out to me.

"The art supplies." He prompted, and I gave him a half smile and took the bag from him.

"Thanks." I peered into the bag for a moment, and when I looked up again, Carter was already gone. Strange.

I shut the door and sat down on the couch, dumping out the stuff next to me. There were a few tubes of paint, one glass jar with something clear inside, an empty jar, a few paintbrushes, and a roll of paper towels. Okay. Maybe I could work with this? Only about half of what I put on the list was here.

I opened the jar up and realized it held white paint. I was a little confused as I looked back at the wall. I had planned to paint a mountain scene, but what good was white paint? The other colors in the tubes were black, yellow and red. I needed to start with at least blue. I looked back down and almost dropped the jar. It was full of blue paint. Holy crap!

What was that Brent said about there being small magic here? I took a deep breath and stared at the jar for a full minute. Might as well use it.

I set the paint on the living room floor and began work on the wall facing the giant window. I began my work on the background, outlining where I planned for the sky to begin and end. My brush was large, but with the amount of wall space I had to work with, it seemed small. Still, I was grateful for the size. The sky wasn't all one color. I filled the empty jar up with water and put it next to me.

After almost three hours of constant working, I stopped. The chimes for dinner had sounded. I hurried to put the almost empty jar of paint down and I shoved the brush into some water before running downstairs.

Somehow, I arrived there before any of the men. The food hadn't even appeared yet on the chairs. I suddenly began to move slowly as I sat down in my usual chair. The plates of food chose that moment to appear with a tiny pop. I sucked in my breath, realizing that there was no way I could deny the magic here for much longer, if at all. The plates of food went to their respective chairs, while mine just hovered in front of me, spinning slowly, as if it knew I was there and it was waiting for me to take it.

For several extensive seconds, I let it stay suspended before I grabbed it out of the air. It was like taking it from a shelf. I put the plate on the ground next to me and put my head in my hands, eyes closed. If magic was possible, why was I just now seeing it? I felt a pressure on my shoulder and looked up, my hair falling in my face. Brent was standing there, his hand resting on my shoulder lightly. I guess I would normally think that he was being creepy, but at that moment, I felt strangely comforted. His eyes held a sympathetic light to them.

He pulled his hand away just moments before Joshua and Carter came in, leaving a warm spot on my shoulder. This time, I made sure I was the only one left in the room after dinner. I wanted to see what would happen to the dishes and chairs once dinner was over. After a little while, the empty plates floated back into the air and dissolved silently into the fire. Slowly, all of the chairs but the one I was using faded away into nothingness. At last, I stood up to leave, and my chair faded away as well.

I went straight to my room and finished rinsing out the left behind paint brush. There was no way I was going to stay awake any longer today. I clearly needed sleep.

~*~

When Alli left the room after lunch, Brent waited a couple seconds before following. He wondered if she would remember that she needed to change the bandages again. He waited in the medical room for a couple minutes before she showed up. Her face was blank as he helped her, and he knew from personal experience that now wasn't the time to talk to her. Nevertheless, he caught her attention before she left the room.

"Just so you know, this place is full of small magic like that." He wondered how she hadn't grown suspicious before now. His words caused her to pause briefly, but after giving him a look that seemed to tell him that she thought he was crazy, she drifted out the door.

Brent immediately went to his mirror to make sure she wasn't going to have another breakdown.

He watched as Carter gave her the art supplies, and as she sorted through them. He watched as the clear stuff turned white and then became sky blue. He watched as she took a deep breath and began to paint. He couldn't see what she was painting, and to some extent that annoyed him. He was curious.

When it was time for the next meal, he tried to get there early, but she was already there. She had her head in her hands, and looked like she wanted to cry. He didn't know why he put a hand on her shoulder. He knew how she felt at that moment, and for some reason, he couldn't find a reason to be angry. He was careful to not alarm her, but she jerked her head up and tensed when she felt his hand. For a second, he thought she would shrink away, but she didn't.

She looked directly into his eyes, and he saw a bewilderment, but not of him. She looked gratefully at him, and it alarmed him. He mentally slapped himself and pulled his hand back, sitting down just as Joshua and Carter appeared. He felt like he was losing whatever sanity he had left.

~*~

The next morning after breakfast, I went back to my living room to find that the glass jar once again held white paint and was completely full. The moment I picked it up, it changed to sky blue again. The sky was almost done, and it was only about an hour more before I finished it. After that, I washed out my brush. When I came back, I found that the color of the paint had changed again and the jar was now full of a dark grey.

This magic concept was definitely going to take a while to get used to.

Chapter 6

Over the next several days, my routine became pretty much the same. I would come out of my room only for meals, skipping every once in a while to paint for a longer period of time. By the end of the week, I had completely covered one of the walls with the mural.

The morning I finished, I let it slip that I was done to Brent.

"That's good." He barely seemed interested in it at all.

"Would you like to see it?" The words came out before I could stop them. Brent seemed a little taken aback by the question, but before I could stammer an apology, he accepted.

"Sure." It was my turn to be startled. I looked at the small amount of food left on my plate and put it down, deciding that I was done. As I stood to leave the room, Brent got up and followed. Out of the corner of my eye, I could see Joshua and Carter staring at us and then back to each other. They looked slightly astonished about something. I chose to ignore them as I left.

I hesitated a little at the door to my room, but I figured that if he had wanted to hurt me, he would have already done it by now. When I entered the living room, I looked over my shoulder to catch a glimpse of Brent's expression. I felt nervous at showing him my work. I had never shown anyone any of it in the past.

Brent gave a half smile as he looked at the mural. It was the closest thing to a real smile that I had seen on him so far. It looked a little strange with the thick scar that ran across his lips since the scar tissue pulled oddly, but it didn't look wrong. It made him seem younger than he looked.

"Do you like it?" Several seconds had passed, and I held my breath, wondering if he found something wrong. I had begun analyzing my own work, finding numerous possible mistakes.

"Yeah. I do like it." He finally turned away and looked at me. His facial mask seemed to crack and he suddenly seemed a bit more human than before. "You paint very well."

"Thanks." I couldn't hold his gaze, so I averted my eyes and stared at the floor instead, glancing up every so often to see if he was still looking at me.

"I think," the sound of his voice got my attention, "that it is time I showed you something as well." He began to walk out of my living room towards the hall. I followed uncertainly, feeling a little confused. This was different.

Brent led me in the direction of the dining room. As we were going down the stairs though, he stopped about halfway down and turned towards me. I suddenly felt nervous all over again. What was he doing?

He barely glanced at me though, studying the wall on the right. He put out a hand and rested it gently on the stone. When he seemed satisfied, he looked back at me and jerked his head as if he wanted me to follow him. Then, he disappeared. It was just like Joshua had done when I first got here.

I stood stock still, staring at the place where he had just been. He had just walked through the wall. Tentatively, I reached out my hand and carefully touched the wall. It was cool to the touch, just as I expected it to be, but as I pressed harder, the tips of my fingers sank into the stone. I jerked my hand quickly back and took a half-step backwards.

Half of Brent's body suddenly came through the stone. It looked very strange seeing one of his legs, an arm, and his head sticking out of the wall. If I weren't freaked out, I would have laughed.

"You don't have to be afraid. Come on." With that, he disappeared once more into the wall. I took a deep breath. I had nothing to lose.

I put my hands in front of me and closed my eyes as I stepped into the wall. The logical part of my brain was screaming at me that I was walking into a potentially painful stone wall, but another small part of me was thrilled at the display of magic.

A cold sensation washed over me temporarily before I felt the familiar warmth of sunlight. My eyes flew open, and I moved one hand

91

to shield them from the light, dropping the other to my side.

I blinked furiously, trying to adjust my eyes to the lighting. As everything came into focus, I caught my breath. I was surrounded by tall trees with a small clearing directly in front of me. I ran a hand along the trunk of a tree to make sure I wasn't in a dream and saw Brent watching me. A small smirk played at the corners of his mouth, and I smiled back at him. I felt so free here!

I swung myself around the trunk of the tree and spun once, looking up at the sky. When I looked back towards Brent, he had an eyebrow raised. I rolled my eyes. That guy had no sense of humor. He had no idea how much I loved the freedom of being outside.

He began to walk through the clearing, so I followed him. I soon found that it ended at the cliffside. Standing on the edge of the cliff, I could just see the town limits in the distance. The view was breathtaking.

"This is amazing." I turned back Brent. "How long have you been coming here?" Before he could answer, I went on. "And what happened with the wall back there? Has it always done that? Is it some kind of portal?"

"Yes." He turned away, leaving me to wonder which question he had just answered. "Follow me," He called over his shoulder.

I had a hard time keeping up with his pace as he strode to the end of the clearing near the edge of the cliff. He kept one arm outstretched, as though searching for something, until he came to such a sudden stop that I ran into his back. He didn't do so much as budge from the impact, whereas I, on the other hand, was thrown backwards and almost slammed my head against a random tree trunk. Who puts trees in the middle of a forest like that anyway?

Brent made sure to glance back to check that I hadn't somehow killed myself when I ran into him. He then proceeded to take a large ball of twine from one of his large jean pockets. One end, he tied to a stray branch that hung slightly over the cliff edge and began to unwind it at about chest high (my head). He hung it over several limbs, walking in a wide semicircle that stretched around the clearing; a total of about sixty feet wide. He seemed to be following something I couldn't see.

"What are you doing?" I asked as I stumbled over sticks and random rocks, trying to follow.

"I'm outlining the boundaries." He stated in a matter of fact tone.

"Okay..." I didn't see where he was going with this.

"Remember how I said that there was magic here? Well, I can only go so far up here. If you go anywhere out of these boundaries, then I can't promise that you will be safe." I paused for a moment in my tracks, making a confused face at his back. Why would I not be safe outside? He turned his head around just in time for him to see me giving him the look.

93

He gave me a deadpan glare, and I ducked my head, biting my lip. Had I gone too far? After a few long seconds, I looked back up, feeling a little irritated with myself for being so scared. Then again, I guess I had a reason to feel that way.

"You know," I began hesitantly, "someday you're going to need to tell me what is going on here. I keep seeing small bits of magic, which seems too good to be true, but the only reason I'm here is because it will keep my family together." I saw a brief flash of anger in his eyes and looked back to the ground before I continued on. "Why am I here?" I asked desperately. "What do you want with me? Why did you strike a deal with me?" I waited for him to reply, but all I heard was footsteps. I looked up quickly, just in time for me to see Brent disappear through a pair of trees. I didn't realize we were so close to the portal. He had left the ball of twine to hang from a tree branch.

What had I said that made him angry enough to leave me alone here? Slowly, I picked up the twine ball from where it had fallen on the ground and put it in the tree. Maybe Brent would come back to finish whatever he was doing.

Wondering if there was something there that I couldn't see, I put my hand out past the hanging string, but my hand never touched anything. There was nothing there.

I shook my head to clear my thoughts, walked back to the edge of the cliff, and leaned against one of the giant trees there. It felt wonderful being outside again. I looked up the tree. Within seconds, I had managed to pull myself up onto one of the branches and began climbing. I settled myself down on the highest branch I could and closed my eyes.

Why did Brent walk away like that? Why was I here? What was the point of me coming to this place?

I had all these questions and absolutely no answers.

I found myself back in my room a few hours later. It was as though the pleasure of finishing the mural this morning had vanished, leaving a dismal cloud over my head. When the signal for lunch rang, I didn't move from my room. I wasn't hungry.

A pounding on my door got me standing. It sounded angry. I was careful to open the door, and I found Brent on the other side with his arms crossed impatiently.

"You're skipping meals again." He spoke slowly, as though he was trying to control himself.

"Why would you care?" I opened the door a bit wider so I could see more. Something flashed in his eyes, and I contemplated shutting the door again.

"You are to join us at meals from now on." Anger flared in me and I moved out of the safety of my room, deciding that the library sounded nice right about now. I tried to keep my anger in check as I moved down the hall. The tone of his voice had sounded hauntingly familiar to a certain boy's that I once knew. Just as I reached the door, I felt a rough hand on my shoulder jerking me around.

"No!" I panicked and tried to pulled away, but he only held on tighter. He was clearly angry.

"I demand-"

"You demand?!" I shouted, unable to control my anger. "You don't own me! You can't demand me to do anything!" I finally twisted out of his steel grip.

"This is not your home and yet you live here! I have a right to-"

"The only reason I live here is because your buddies down there trapped me in an impossible situation! If not for you, I wouldn't ever be here, for any reason! Oh, and I still don't know why I'm here, but I guess it doesn't matter, because my family is 'supposedly' safe! If it's a normal thing for you to do this to young girls, then you are sick! My family is at my home, but I'm here, and it's all your fault!" As I ranted, I watched as gradually Brent's face got colder and harder. His eyes practically burning with anger. He moved an arm up sharply, almost as if he was going to hit me, and I realized that I could be in so much trouble if I stayed where I was.

I turned around, suddenly full of fright, and ran. I ran down the rest of the hallway and practically flew down the stairs, skimming my hand along the wall to find the opening. As soon as I found it, I threw my body against the stone. I picked myself up from the dirty ground of the forest and ran to the same tree I had climbed earlier.

By the time Brent appeared outside, I was already high enough in the tree where he couldn't see me. My body was physically shaking as he looked everywhere, even scanning some of the trees for me. For one scary moment, I thought he had seen me, but then he turned away. My pounding heart began to slow when he finally turned and disappeared through the portal.

After a tense several minutes, I made my way down the limbs and slide down to sit at the base of the trunk. My mind felt numb after what had just happened. I had just shouted at a man who could very easily kill me, and now he was searching for me. Great! It was only noon, and yet I already felt drained. I couldn't find the energy to run right now, so I ended up with my head buried in my arms as time slipped away.

I was terrified.

~*~

"I think," Brent watched Allison's eyes snap up to meet his as he spoke, "that it is time I showed you something as well." He headed out of the room, knowing that she would follow. He was correct when a couple seconds later, her footsteps could be heard echoing behind his. He had been debating showing her how to reach the outside premises for a while. He hated the fact that she viewed him as a prison warden of some kind, and he was kind of hoping that she would at least not hate him.

He led her to the stairway, stopping halfway down it. He tried to ignore how she flinched when he turned around. Fear had flooded her eyes and any confidence she had in him had left, leaving her looking uncertain.

97

He located the portal entrance and stepped through, jerking his head once for her to follow. To be honest, he couldn't wait to see what Allison's reaction to this would be. He knew that to her it would look as though he had just walked through a wall. He saw the tips of her fingers appear in midair, but they quickly disappeared. Brent smiled to himself. She was probably completely stunned. He knew he was when he found out how it worked. Joshua had "accidentally" tripped him and he had fallen through, landing among a bunch of trees. Unfortunately for Joshua, all he could see was a pair of legs sticking out of a completely solid wall, still moving. To say that Joshua had freaked out was an understatement.

Neither Joshua nor Carter had been able to follow Brent outside. He was the only one who could go to the top of the cliff. But apparently other people could follow. This had been discovered when a girl had accidentally stumbled across the entrance. She had disappeared the next day.

But now, watching Allison figure out how the portal worked made Brent want to laugh at how timid she was. He stuck half of his body back through to reassure her.

"You don't have to be afraid. Come on." He almost smiled just then at the uncertain look on her face, but he disappeared before she could see it. Part of him wondered why he was doing this, if it meant she would just leave. But then again, she had stayed this long and she could leave whenever she chose to.

When Allison walked through the portal with both hands extended and both eyes shut tightly, he had to hold back his laughter. She was so amazed that she was outside, that when she ended up spinning, he had to raise an eyebrow. She was acting completely different that just five seconds before. It was as if a weight had been lifted off of her chest. When she rolled her eyes, he knew something was different. She had just rolled her eyes at him without a trace of fear. Amazing.

He turned away and walked into the clearing. Allison followed and moved straight past him to the cliff edge. She stood almost exactly where he normally would sit to pass time.

"It's amazing." She finally spoke. "How long have you been coming here?" Brent wondered how he should reply, but she just went right on with the questions before he could pull together a suitable answer. All he ended up hearing was, "...Is it some kind of portal?"

"Yes." Brent settled for just answering that one question as he turned away. He was looking for the boundary. It should be very near the giant tree with a long limb hanging over the cliff edge. When his hand hit the invisible wall, he stopped, unable to go any farther. A millisecond later, Allison rammed into his back, and he glanced over his shoulder. She seemed to be completely fine as she glared slightly at a tree as if didn't belong in the forest. He just rolled his eyes as he took a ball of twine out of his pocket that he had put there early this morning before breakfast. He had been planning to do this without her here, but the situation had changed.

He began to mark out the boundary as well as he could without ramming his hand into the barrier. Although the wall was invisible, it felt like cement. He made it about fifteen feet before Allison started questioning him.

"What are you doing?"

He tried to figure out how to explain this to her. "I'm outlining the boundaries." Maybe if he sounded sure enough she would just take his word for it and not ask anything else.

"Okay..." She didn't sound convinced at all. He mentally sighed and tried to explain to the best of his abilities.

"Remember how I said that there was magic here? Well, I can only go so far up here. If you go anywhere out of these boundaries, then I can't promise that you will be safe."

Brent wasn't sure how that came across, so he glanced back at Allison. She looked like she was either confused or making faces at him. He wasn't sure which was true, so he gave her a look.

When she responded by looking at the ground and biting her lip, he almost groaned out loud. He liked it better when she didn't seem completely terrified of him.

"You know," Allison began to finally speak, looking at his face at last, "someday you're going to need to tell me what is going on here. I keep seeing signs of magic, which seems too good to be true, but the only reason I'm here is because it will keep my family together."

Brent felt his chest tighten at her words. If she was trying to make him angry, it was certainly working. She had looked away again.

She kept talking to him, but he couldn't hear anymore of her words. He felt as though he could barely control himself. He had to get away from her. The ball of twine fell from his fingers as he made his way inside a quickly as possible without breaking into a run.

By the time he reached his room, he wanted to hit something. He had really gone out on a limb by trusting her with the knowledge of how to go outside and not run away. He even tried to show that he cared about her safety, but then she turned around and blamed him for holding her captive!

He jerked open the door to the room with the mirror and snarled a command out as quickly as he could, not wishing to see his reflection longer than needed. He stared at the fogged glass, wondering how far she had managed to go so far, but to his surprise, she was still. She was sitting on a tree branch with her back against the trunk and her eyes closed. The only indication that she wasn't asleep was the small frown she wore. She looked troubled.

He cut the connection.

When she didn't show up for lunch, he checked the mirror again, unable to stop himself from wondering where she could be by this time. She wasn't outside at all. She was curled up on the

101

couch in her room, staring blankly at her mural. He found himself relieved that she was still here, but at the same time, he was tired of this. She couldn't keep spending her days not eating and watching a wall.

He went to her room and banged on her door. She opened it a crack, barely meeting his eye. He crossed his arms.

"You're skipping meals again."

"Why do you care?" She spoke softly, even though there was a hint of anger in her voice. As though she even had the right to be angry.

"You are to join meals from now on." She opened her door all of the way, but she completely ignored him. She brushed past him, heading towards the library. Brent's anger flared up. Even now it seem as though she was trying to infuriate him. He stopped her from entering the library. She had to stop doing these things.

"No!" She jerked under his grip, and glared at him, responding to his own anger. There was no hint of fear. Who did she think she was?

"I demand-" Of course she cut him off.

"You demand?!" She was shouting. "You don't own me! You can't demand me to do anything!" She jerked away.

"This is not your home and yet you live here! I have a right to-" Now he was shouting. Great. He really needed to get away before he did something he regretted. She cut him off again though, and he abandoned the idea of walking away.

"The only reason I live here is because your buddies down there trapped me in an impossible situation! If not for you, I wouldn't ever be here, for any reason! Oh, and I still don't know why I'm here, but I guess it doesn't matter, because my family is 'supposedly' safe! If it's a normal thing for you to do this to young girls, then you are sick! My family is at my home and I'm here and it's all your fault!" Brent could feel himself closing off to the world as she continued. He knew that what she said was true. His anger reached a breaking point and he threw his hand up in exasperation and took a deep breath. He wasn't going to hit her, but he knew the moment he had shifted that he had made a mistake.

Allison's eye had gone from anger to pure fear within seconds. He had never seen her look so scared in the whole time she had been here. A large part of him wondered what exactly was going through her head in that brief second, but another much smaller part of him already knew that she expected the worst.

She ran. He knew that if it was her choice she would never come back, but he chased her anyway. He didn't know what he would say. His anger had been cut off by that look of fear. If anything, he should apologize. If only he knew what to say.

He knew as soon as he ran into the dining area that she hadn't come that way. Joshua and Carter looked up in confusion as he ran in and then ran right back out. Brent went outside. It was the only place she could have gone.

But there was nothing out there. He could neither hear nor see anyone. She was gone.

It didn't matter.

At least, that was what he told himself as he went to his room. He refused to even look in the mirror. It was over. He was done. He could finally give up on the idea of ever living a normal life. He was relieved that Allison was gone. Now she wouldn't have to live with a monster. And he would remain one. He hated his life.

Chapter 7

Darkness. My eyes snapped open to the darkness of the night.

I must have somehow fallen asleep leaning against the tree. There was no telling how much time had passed, but judging from the growling of my stomach, I had definitely missed dinner. I slowly uncurled from my sitting position and shakily got to my feet. Why I had woken up, I had no idea. I scanned the dark forest around me, but there didn't seem to be anything around.

I walked away from where I knew the portal entrance had to be. When my head suddenly touched something hanging from the trees, I had to hold back a scream. I was first relieve and then annoyed to find that it was just the string that Brent had strung around the clearing. I ducked under it and saw off to my left, away from the cliff side, the light of what seemed to be a campfire. I thought about it for a moment before picking my way toward the light.

There was no way I was going to go back to that place if I could help it. Maybe I could find help getting home. I'm sure I could figure out how to keep my family together without Joshua, Carter, and Brent's deal.

About thirty yards away from the fire, I rammed my knee into a very hard wooden post with some signs on it. Frowning, I ran my hand over it, finding that there were several deeply carved letters in the wood. The only place that I knew around here that had wooden signs everywhere was... I knew where I was suddenly. This had to be that nearby state park: Johanna something-or-other. I didn't really know what the name was, but it sounded something like that. If I was in a state park, then that fire must be from some campers! A sense of relief flooded my body, and I began to hurry to the campsite.

As I go closer to the firelight, I began to make out voices. I hesitated about ten yards back as I observed the people around the fire. From what I could see, they were all men. I took that to be a bad sign. I had hoped to see some family vacationing instead. The longer I observed them, the more I began to notice strange things. Like the fact that they all seemed to have guns. I'd rather risk going back to Brent than risk guns. I did *not* like guns.

By now, I was pretty far outside the boundary line that Brent had begun to set up, so I slowly worked my way backwards. Of course, that meant that I had to accidentally step on a large, very dry stick. It snapped in half loudly, and a deadly silence fell upon the night. Of course that would happen to me.

I jerked my head up as the men around the campfire all looked in my direction. I didn't wait for them to spot me before I ran as fast as I could back to the portal. This was not good. Not good at all.

I raced in the direction of Brent's clearing, knowing that I would be safe there. As I ran, I knew exactly where I needed to go in order to get inside. About thirty yards in front of me, I could see a faint light that stretched across the tree line. Almost the moment I noticed this though, something very solid and very hard slammed into me, knocking me to the ground. All of the air was pushed from my lungs, leaving me gasping on the forest floor.

Before I knew it, I was being pulled up and back through the trees toward the fire. I was still catching my breath when I felt a cold hand grab my chin and force my eyes to meet theirs. I suddenly caught my breath. There was no humanly way that it was possible.

"My, oh my. What do we have here? What are the chances? I mean, really?" The harsh voice was way too familiar. My father's "associate" still sounded as though he smoked a pack a day. He laughed as he saw my eyes grow wider. "What? Sorry to see me? I can't tell whether or not I agree with that." He let go of me. Now I got a chance to see around me. Besides Rasp, there was Sile and one other man that I had never seen before.

"Now. To figure out what to do with her." The man holding me spoke. I dubbed him Creep.

"You can have your fun later. What I want to know is why you are here." Rasp addressed the last part to me.

"I swear I didn't know you were here! I didn't-" My frantic words were cut off when Rasp backhanded me. The force snapped my head to the side, and I gasped in surprise and pain. It felt like he had hit me with a sledgehammer.

Rasp laughed, but it sounded cold and distant.

"You act as though we care about your stories. Well, hear me clearly." He grabbed hold of my chin and smiled cruelly when he saw me flinch. "I couldn't care less." He let me go and stood back a little. "Now. The truth. Is this about your father? Did he send you?"

"N-No! He's in prison." My tone took on a slightly hollow ring, and Rasp looked at me for a moment.

"This is interesting." His voice was suddenly calm, and it freaked me out. It was like listening to a horror movie narrator. "Of course your daddy isn't in prison." He paused as though thinking. "Ah! I know." He let out a low laugh. "You can tell that father of yours that he'll get no help from us. We don't need the police after us too."

I suddenly connected the dots. Dad must be on the run from the authorities. Oh Lord, he was in so much trouble. I groaned mentally at his actions. He had better not do anything that could endanger Mom or Dan.

"I do-" I cut myself off, realizing that I should have just agreed with the man. If I had, they might have let me go, but there was no way they would now.

"Alright. So you didn't know." Rasp drew closer. "Who sent you?"

"I was telling the truth before! I didn't know you were here! I thought that you might just be camp-" This time it wasn't a hand, but cold metal that came out of nowhere and struck me. I felt my knees give out, and Creep let go, allowing me to sink to the ground. There was no way I was going to be moving just then. I refused to let out a sound as I felt a small trickle of warmth fall down my face. I reached up a shaking hand, and sure enough, it came away red and sticky with blood.

"No more games." I snapped up my throbbing head and jerked back at the sight of the gun. My hands groped for whatever was behind me. I latched onto a pitifully small stick and swung it. I managed to knock the gun out of Rasp's hand temporarily, no thanks to the stick. After that, my luck was gone. I didn't even manage to stand up before Creep grabbed me. That small stunt earned me another painful connection to the head. I couldn't help the wounded cry that escaped from my lips as my eyes watered, tears finally falling in small streams.

Rasp finally recovered the gun, anger blazing in his eyes. Without another word, he raised up the gun. I squeezed my eyes shut tightly. This was definitely not how I imagined dying. I just prayed to God that it would be over soon.

Chapter 8

Brent skipped dinner that night. Alli's habit must have started to rub off on him. The irony.

Joshua and Carter had given up banging on his door, trying to get him to come out, hours ago. They had obviously pieced together what had happened. Now the silence was deafening.

Brent's eyes focus back on the mirror once more. He wanted so badly to know if she had made it to her home. It was a desire that had been developed over a year ago. She wasn't the first girl, although she would be the last. He rubbed his face tiredly and spoke before he could stop himself again.

"Show me Alli."

His reflection melted away into darkness for a moment before blurred figures filled the glass.

"...camp-!" His ear picked up on the last words off a desperate sentence. That wasn't right. The image in the mirror cleared just in time for Brent to see the barrel of a gun ram into the side of Allison's head. Brent jerked into an alert sitting position as she fell to the ground. He noted that she was in the forest.

"No more games!" Brent was gone from the room long before the man finished speaking.

~*~

Death never came. My eyes flew open just in time to see the gun ripped from Rasp's hand by someone I knew all too well.

Within seconds, Brent had knocked him out. While he was doing this, Sile and Creep drew their guns and quickly aimed at Brent.

"Watch out!" I shouted as Brent turned to face Sile next. A second later, a loud gunshot echoed in the forest. I naturally screamed as Brent jerked and bent over, clutching his shoulder in pain.

"Shut up!" Creep spoke harshly in my ear. "Don't move!" Creep pointed his gun to my head and shouted Brent, who immediately stopped in his tracks. "I don't care who goes first, but she does if you move." I was stunned that Brent was still standing. There was blood covering the majority of his left arm and it was soaking into his shirt. He looked frightening, but all I wanted to do was run to him for protection.

I took a risk then that I would probably look back at and regret. I twisted my body as hard as I could, slamming my head into Creep's with a sickening crack. Blood immediately came pouring from it, and Creep's grip loosened a little. It was just enough for me to try to jerk the gun from his grip, but he just threw me off.

I hit the side of a tree and then the ground, all in a daze. As much as this only added to my pain, it provided the distraction needed for Brent to knock Sile unconscious and get close enough to send the gun in Creep's hand flying away.

After that, it was a mad struggle to reach the fallen gun. Each time Creep reached out, Brent managed to kick the weapon farther away. In return, Creep would do his best to knock Brent out, but it was rare that he managed to land any of his punches.

When the gun was suddenly pushed near me, I quickly grabbed it and tried to hurl it away. Before I could, someone crashed into me. I would have hit the ground hard if that person hadn't wrapped his arms around me and twisted just in time. I heard a dull crack as I landed on top of Brent, who gave out a slightly strangled cry and immediately pushed me off of him. I rolled about five feet away from him. The gun had long since vanished.

Before I could recover, someone's arm pressed down on my neck, cutting off my airway. Above me, I could see the form of Creep almost directly over me. I struggled harder when I noticed that he had a knife with him, but that just made my vision go darker as I started to black out.

Had I been rescued from death, only to die a couple seconds later?

Another loud gunshot resounded in the forest.

Moments later, Creep's body fell directly across my stomach, the knife falling from his hand. I gasped for breath, feeling like drowning man coming up for air. What...

I glanced up just in time to see Brent fall down to his knees, gasping for breath. He was alive, which was much better than the alternative.

I felt like letting myself stay where I was, but first I needed to get out from under Creep. His body was practically crushing my ribs. When I managed to do so, I moved as fast as I could toward Brent, who had collapsed. I knelt over him and made sure he hadn't stopped breathing. All of his scars stood out in an angry red against the rest of his skin. To be honest, it looked more disturbing than before. His face was drawn in pain and as pale as a sheet. I carefully pulled his hand away from his shoulder, but stopped when he let out a deep groan of pain.

"Brent?" I waited for a moment for a reply, before trying to slide my arm under his back to help him sit up. He left out another groan at the movement and opened his eyes. I held my breath slightly when he looked at me, agony in his eyes.

"Does this amount of trouble always follow you around?" With that, his head lolled back over. I was shocked frozen. Had he seriously just made a joke at a time like this? Brent had never once made a joke or even attempted to be humorous, but now that he was probably dying, he cracked a joke? Wow. I didn't know what to think.

Once I shook off the shock, I did my best to wake Brent up. It didn't work out too well. He was out cold and was a whole lot heavier than he looked. There was no way that I would be able to get him to the portal by myself.

114

Now that I thought about it, I had no idea where the portal was. We were lost in the forest, at least until morning. Now that the adrenaline of the past half hour or so had worn off, I was exhausted, and I began to realize just how much blood was coming out of Brent. I was suddenly thankful that Brent wasn't awake as I removed his hand from his shoulder. He was in for a world of hurt. My stomach twisted itself into knots as I realized that he was still bleeding profusely. I blinked rapidly and did my best to push down the rising nausea, but it didn't help much.

When I knew that I couldn't hold it down much longer, I jerked away from my position next to Brent and got as far away as I could before I threw up what was left of both breakfast and dinner from the previous night. When I finally stopped, I tried to get the horrible taste out of my mouth. This was going to be a long night.

I got back to Brent as fast as I could. One of the first things I noticed when I could think clearly was that the bullet had gone all of the way through his shoulder. It must have just barely missed the bone.

Before I could think much about what I was doing, I undid his shirt and pulled the cloth away from the wound. It was still bleeding, so I did the best I could to pull the rest of his shirt off to use to block the blood flow. In a nutshell, I felt very awkward.

After applying pressure to his wound, I bound the shirt around his shoulder as tightly as I

115

could, but I kept additional pressure on it, just in case. My mind had grown numb. I could barely register the fact that my hands were covered in dried blood. I did my best to avoid looking at Brent altogether, but it was hard to not notice the giant scar that knotted across his chest and torso. It was about as thick as my wrists and was the origin of several other branching scars. There was no way that he had gotten those by an accident. I had to pull my eyes away from the horrific sight. They settled on his side where a giant purple and blue bruise was forming. I realized that it was a result of our fall. There had been a dull crack when we hit the ground. If my guess was true, Brent could have several broken ribs right now. Great. The night just had to get better, didn't it?

It took just a little longer to realize my own pain and exhaustion. My head was killing me and in the firelight, I could make out several bruises that dotted my own body. I definitely hadn't broken anything, but it sure felt like it. My whole body hurt.

Holding one hand over Brent's wound, I gently touched the side of my head. There were two goose eggs there, but they were no longer bleeding. As my hand brushed my cheek, I guessed that there was a hand shaped bruise there, judging by the tenderness.

About a half hour slipped away before I attempted to get Brent to wake up. I was pretty sure by then that Creep was dead, but I couldn't tell with Rasp or Sile. It didn't matter much to me. I had

116

already spent way longer than I wished to in their presence.

"Brent!" I shook his good shoulder. Hopefully it didn't hurt too much. "Come on, Brent!" I saw his eyes twitch, and after a little more urging on my part, he let out a moan of pain. "Come on! I need your help to do this." I slid an arm under him and began to try to lift him into a sitting position.

"S-stop." He barely managed to get the words out.

"I'm sorry, but we need to get to Joshua and Carter." It was slow process, getting him to sit up all of the way, but at last, leaning heavily on me, he managed to get to his feet.

Now, I just had to make sure to go in the right direction. I scanned the forest line for that same glow that I had seen before. I was sure that if I could find it, I could get to the right place.

Brent was slowly becoming more aware of our circumstance. I believed it was the pain that caused his awareness. I just hoped that he wasn't going to pass out from it again. I scanned the forest more desperately. Where was it?

A bright light flashed faintly in the distance, and I could suddenly see a steady glow through the trees. There it was.

Brent used his good arm to lean on me, and I kept an arm around his torso as we slowly made our way to the light. The closer we got, the more of the light I could see. I found that it wasn't a lamp or candle, but rather the light emanated from a dimly lit wall. Maybe this was the boundary that Brent

117

had mentioned before? At this point, I couldn't tell if I was hallucinating or not. I wasn't sure how much longer Brent could stay awake, but he had surprised me before. He would probably do it again.

Still, I couldn't help but hesitate before I walked through the thin, translucent wall. The logical part of my brain that still worked was telling me I was going to hit my head even harder, but the other part either knew better or didn't care enough.

When I stepped through, there was no distinct sensation, only a slight warmth; it was the same warmth that I had always experienced after returning home after being away for a while. Once past the wall, I could see better, and the night air seemed lighter. There was another light, more pale and dim than the boundary, between two tall trees just ten yards away. Thank God!

A cool sensation swept over me as we stepped through the portal, and I almost collapsed then and there, but I couldn't with Brent still relying on me. My head began to throb worse than before, and a heavy tiredness was stealing over me.

"Joshua! Carter! We need help!" I took a deep breath, glancing up at Brent. I could just make him out in the dark hallway. Seriously, that guy had lost so much blood by now; I'm surprised that he hadn't fallen over again. "Anytime right about now would be helpful!" I was practically screaming and my voice broke several times from exhaustion.

Within seconds, both Joshua and Carter rounded the corner of the stairs. They took one look at Brent, and the weight on my shoulders

118

disappeared. They must not have seen how I looked yet.

I struggled to follow Joshua and Carter, leaning on the wall for support, as they helped get Brent to the medical room. I would need some help as soon as we were sure that he wouldn't die from blood loss. I had no idea if I was hurt in any serious way at all, but I was almost positive that I had a concussion.

Inside the medical room, Joshua and Carter got Brent to lie down on the table, the moonlight and several lit torches revealed the extent of Brent's injuries. The bullet had torn through the muscle tissue of his shoulder, exiting the other side. It had probably grazed his bone. There was blood everywhere. His shirt was practically soaked with it when they removed it from his shoulder. I almost threw up again when I saw the blood so clearly once more.

After a few deep breaths, I grabbed some paper towels and got them wet. I brought them to Brent, trying not to stare at the blood. Carter was supporting Brent while Joshua was doing his best to quickly wrap Brent's ribs.

"Here." Joshua handed me a thin cloth. "Put pressure on the wound with it." I almost couldn't believe my ears. Now probably wasn't the time to mention that I hated the sight of blood. But still, I did my best. The moment I touched the cloth to Brent's shoulder, he pulled away, and Carter glared at me as though it was my fault. It probably was.

119

"You just need to hold still." I steeled myself and pressed it over the hole, trying to think happy thoughts. Brent jerked harder than before, using his good arm to push me away. The force propelled me against the stone wall not far away. He must have been more awake now than he had been outside.

"Leave me alone!" If I thought Brent was scary in the past, him shouting at me while I was already in pain and past the point of exhaustion made me want to crawl into a hole and die. "You've done enough for now!" I tried to blink back tears, staying as far back in a dark shadow so he couldn't have the satisfaction of seeing me cry.

"If you would just hold still, it won't hurt so much-" He cut off my strained words.

"I think you've done enough." He grimaced in discomfort, trying to push away Carter's help with support. "If you hadn't run away, this wouldn't have happened!"

"And who caused me to run away?" I spoke softly, wiping away a hot tear that managed to escape my eye. When I touched my head, I cringed when my hand accidentally brushed against the swollen knot where the gun had twice hit me. I made sure there wasn't any blood on my hand before I looked up again at the sound of Brent hissing in pain.

Joshua had taken the discarded towel and was now pressing it against Brent's shoulder for me. I noticed that he whispered something harshly into Brent's ear. Brent was looking at me, but his eyes were no longer angry. He looked strangely sympathetic.

"I'm sorry." I could barely hear his voice, but he sounded as though he meant it. I nodded slowly to show that I heard him. I went over to the medical cabinet and looked in it. There was nothing there but a few thin towels. There was a list of instructions on the door, but there wasn't anything in the cabinet itself. I glanced over the instructions, but they made no sense whatsoever.

"Umm..." I turned back to the men. Joshua was looking at me expectantly, holding pressure on the wound, while Carter was supporting Brent. I addressed Joshua. "I don't understand the instructions. They keep saying something about petals and sand."

Brent's eyes snapped open at the information, looking at me sharply.

"Read them to me word for word." His voice took a hard tone to it that made me nervous, but I did what he said.

"Chew a single petal within ten seconds of picking and rub about a teaspoon of the top layer of the sand over the wound openings." I looked back at Brent, but he had his eyes closed and had stopped fighting to sit up straight. The blood loss seemed to have taken its toll on him. After a bit, he opened his eyes and looked at me again.

"Anything else?" I ran my eyes back over the instructions, finally resting them on a note near the bottom.

"There's a note at the bottom. 'Sorry about the dosage. There was too much muscle damage. Plus, those broken ribs didn't help. Don't worry too much.' There's some symbol at the bottom, but no name." When I looked back up, Brent was struggling to sit back up. If he had broken ribs, no wonder he was in so much pain. "Stay still! You could..." I moved closer to Brent, but Joshua held up an arm.

"If I don't get to my room, I may never be able to use my arm properly ever again." Brent seemed to know exactly what the note had meant. Carter and Joshua helped Brent get to his feet, and I followed them out of the medical room. That guy was something.

When we reached Brent's door, Joshua quickly opened it, and then looked at Carter and Brent with annoyance. Joshua slammed his fist on something that stopped his hand from passing through the doorway. Carter rolled his eyes, and Brent groaned.

"What?" I looked between the three of them. I put out a hand to see if there was something that I was missing, but there was nothing there. Again. "Is something wrong?"

Joshua addressed me. "Carter and I can't go into Brent's room. But apparently you can." The last part he mumbled under his breath, but I still caught it.

"Guys. Can we please talk a little less?" Brent spoke more tired than before, and we looked at him. He made as if to move by himself, but he looked like the walking dead. He wasn't going anywhere. Carter rolled his eyes again before practically dumping Brent on top of me.

"Help him." He then gave both of us a push towards the stairs that led to Brent's room. I almost fell down right then and there, and grabbed at Brent for support, which was stupid. The guy could barely stand on his own right now. Both of us ended up hitting the wall. Brent let out a groan and clutched his side. I had to make sure he didn't fall over while doing so.

"Really?" I shot at Carter before Brent could speak. I could barely see straight now, my head was throbbing so badly. Brent looked ready to punch Carter's lights out in spite of being physically unable to at the moment. I saw Joshua hit him in the back of the head for Brent.

As I helped support Brent up the stairs, I was almost surprised by how similar it was to me helping him outside. Only, now he was more awake. I looked up at Brent briefly. Or maybe not.

His stairs were a lot less steep than mine were and went on longer. With no light, I kept thinking that I was about to run into something. When we came to the end of the stairs, I had to admit that I was surprised by Brent's room. For some reason, I had half expected it to be full of sharp tools and torture devices. It was lit by a single torch on the wall next to the door. I could see three other doors in the room and a couple of unlit torches at various places on the wall. There was almost nothing in the room but a single bed.

"Where do I go?" Brent motioned as best he could toward a door on my left. When I tried to open it though, I found that it was locked. I couldn't find any visible lock on the door. I looked up at Brent, who had just managed to finish rolling his eyes.

"Look up." I did and saw that there was a deadbolt at the top of the door. If Brent could hear my thoughts right then, I honestly wondered how he might react. I quickly unlocked the door and opened it.

At first, I had to blink at the sudden light, but as my eyes adjusted, I found that it was actually quite dim. The room itself was relatively small, but it seemed larger than it was because of what was at the center. There, inside of a small glass pot, a thin stem poked out of the dirt with four rose petals on it. One was mostly withered and brown, while the other three petals were perfectly fine. Above the almost dead flower was a small ball of light that seemed to be made up of particles of either sand or dust.

The flower might have been beautiful at one point, but now... The sight of it seemed to strike a chord in me that signaled something awful was about to happen.

"Pick one of the good petals." Brent's voice pulled me out of my trance, and I stared at him for a moment before obeying his words. His voice was no longer calm and controlled, but filled with pain and perhaps a little fear. His eyes seemed to betray the bit of fear in them as well, but I couldn't tell, because I had seen very little emotion in them so far.

"Okay." I said softly, more than a little unsure as to why he had to do this. It felt wrong to pick the petal off the dying flower. Almost the moment my fingers touched one of the petals, it fell off of the flower. Brent moved his arm from around my shoulder and took the petal. I cautiously watched him to make sure he wasn't going to pass out or anything. He ate the petal quickly before putting his hand back on my shoulder. He was shaking, even though his grip on me was hard. I winced at the pressure, but didn't move.

I waited, uncertain as to what to do next. Brent rested for a moment before attempting to carefully pinch some of the soil from the thin glass pot. When his finger gently brushed the stem on accident, he jerked back quickly as to not damage it.

"What do I do?" I realized he couldn't do it himself.

"You read the instructions." He spoke in a slightly strained voice. "Take about a teaspoon of the topsoil and press it against each bullet hole." I know that I had already read these instructions on the cabinet, but where were they coming from? "Just do it." Brent's tired voice brought me out of my musing. I let go of Brent and he carefully stood back from me and sat down heavily on the floor so I could reach his shoulder better. I carefully took some of the top sand from the pot. I could just feel the tops of some of the thin white roots of the flower. This made me all the more cautious.

125

I took enough sand in the palm of my hand to cover both bullet openings and knelt next to Brent. I took off the blood-soaked towels and recoiled at the sight of so much blood. The wound was still bleeding. I pinched half of what I had in my hand and pressed it over the center of the blood flow.

"Harder." I almost didn't hear Brent. I closed my eyes and did what he said. A few seconds later, he reminded me to do it to the other side as well. I opened my eyes just barely enough to see what I was doing before closing them again as I applied the pressure.

Several thoughts were going through my head. I was crazy. This was crazy. There was a lot of blood. This must be very painful for Brent. I was alone with Brent in a darkish room. I was never going to escape this place. Another thought flashed by. Brent came to save my life, even though I ran away from him.

Brent's muscle grew tenser under my hands the longer I kept them there. Suddenly, the tension that had slowly built up disappeared.

"Okay." Brent's voice came softly. I pulled away, opening my eyes. There was still so much blood on him, the floor, and on my hands. I sat down completely, pushing myself against the wall.

Brent slowly moved his injured arm around, stretching it as if there was nothing wrong with it. He took the discarded towels and did his best to wipe away the blood. My breath caught in my throat as I realized that the hole where the bullet had entered and exited his skin was gone. All that remained was a faint silvery scar.

I looked down at my hands, my head filling with pain at the sharp movement. They still had blood all over them. Now that I thought about it, the pain came at full force. A couple tears slipped out of the corner of my eyes that I didn't bother to wipe away. My mind tried to comprehend everything that had happened. It couldn't.

I looked up at Brent just in time to see him turn to me. There was an empty sadness in his eyes. A sob caught in my throat. If this was magic, then it scared me. I buried my face in my arms and let my emotions take over. A few second later, I felt strong, warm arms encircle me. I cried into Brent, completely undone.

Several minutes later, after I had calmed down a bit, I felt an arm shift under me and lift me up. I could feel the movements but I had already allowed myself to fall asleep too deeply to react.

Chapter 9

When Brent got shot, the only thought that immediately registered was how much pain there was. He had seen movies before when the good guy got shot, but continued to fight anyway as though nothing had happened. This was not like that at all. There was pain. And a LOT of it.

The second thought that registered was that Alli was screaming. Oh. Right. She was going to die. Right.

He straightened back up when Alli went silent, doing his absolute best to ignore the majority of his brain that was screaming at him that his arm felt like it was going to fall off.

"Don't move! I don't care who goes first, but she does if you move." The man, who was holding Alli, held a gun to her head. Of course, Brent stopped moving. There were two men left. One was restraining Alli, while the other fumbled with a gun in his back pocket. Brent took this time to see what Alli's condition was. She had obviously been hit several times, judging from the bruises on her and the blood on one side of her face. Her eyes begged him to save her.

He had no idea how he was going to do that, but Alli seemed to be able to read his mind. She chose that moment to attempt escaping, giving the other guy a bloody nose in the process. She ended getting thrown into a tree for her efforts, but it gave Brent the time he needed to knock out the man not holding Alli and tackle the guy with the gun to the ground. The gun flew from the man's hand, and Brent was determined to keep it that way.

Brent did his best to keep from getting in the way of the guy's fists, but sometimes it was just too hard to manage. The agonizing pain that was radiating from his shoulder didn't help. He could barely focus as it was.

The other guy got a good kick against his chest that knocked the air out of his lungs and sent him stumbling backwards. Brent crashed into Alli, sending them both towards the ground. He barely had time to twist his body around before they hit the ground. It was then that Brent heard the dull crack and cried out as he felt even more pain flash up his ribcage. Oh, God, he felt like he was dying. He shoved Alli off of his chest, trying to get air of any sort into his lungs.

He could barely see straight, but when there is a man standing over the girl next to you, choking her with a knife raised, it's kind of hard to not notice. Right. Gun. He jerked to his feet almost mechanically and his hand closed over the handle as Alli let out a loud scream. He raised it and pulled the trigger, almost without thinking.

The gunshot left a strange silence in the forest. Brent sank down, doing his best to gulp air. He had just killed a man. Alli was safe. He was in so much pain. It hurt to breath. Spots danced before his eyes as he fell back. He closed his eyes. Yep! The ground felt so much better right now.

A sudden flash of pain from his shoulder caused him to groan. He couldn't tell if Alli had called out his name or not. A cool arm slid under his good shoulder and began to cause him to sit up. Ribs. Ow. He groaned again and opened his eyes. Couldn't he just pass out already? It didn't take long for his eyes to find Alli. At the current moment, all he could recognize about her was her dark hair.

"Does this amount of trouble always follow you around?" He managed to get those sardonic words out before finally welcoming oblivion.

~*~

Pain seemed to be everywhere.

"Come on, Brent!" Pain. The cool arm was back, trying to lift him up.

"S-stop." That hurt. He just wanted to be left alone. Maybe the pain would leave eventually if he ignored it long enough. Probably not, but it was worth a shot.

A voice said something about Joshua and Carter. He tried to ignore it too, but that was easier thought than done. Eventually, he found that he didn't have the strength to argue, and he let the cool arm pull him into a sitting position.

His ribs felt like fire. As the voice and the cool arms pulled him to his feet, he realized that it

131

had to be Alli. Her arms were wrapped around him, keeping him standing. Soon, they were also moving slowly in the darkness. He almost collapsed when he took the first step, but she was there to help. He hoped she knew the way back home.

The darkness was endless. He immediately knew they were close when a rush of warmth covered him. The warmth allowed him to breathe easier and become more aware of what was around him. Unfortunately, it also isolated the pain that filled his body to his shoulder and ribs.

By the time they had gotten inside, Brent was ready to pass out again. Alli shouted for Joshua and Carter until the two finally reached them. The cool arms disappeared from around him as Joshua and Carter lifted him.

It wasn't until a sharp jolt of pain when through his shoulder that he realized what was going on. He pulled away from the pressure Alli was trying to apply to the wound.

"You just need to hold still." She sounded a little lightheaded herself.

When she pressed the cloth she was holding to his shoulder even harder than before, he physically shoved her away. She just didn't get it.

"Leave me alone! You've done enough for now!" Anger coursed through him. Why couldn't she just listen to one thing?

"If you would just hold still, it won't hurt so much-" He cut her off again.

"I think you've done enough." His voice was hard and cold. He didn't want anyone's help right now. He tried to push Carter away. "If you hadn't run away, this wouldn't have happened!" He spoke harshly, and honestly wasn't expecting her to reply again.

"And who caused me to run away?" Her voice was so quiet, he almost didn't hear it, but he could see. She was mostly hidden by shadows, but a thin sliver of light revealed several small streams of dried blood on her cheek. She had tear streaks down her face, and when she tried to wipe them away, he saw her face twist in pain. He realized that several of the shadows on her face were actually bruises forming.

He also grimaced in pain as Joshua pressed some towels to the wound harder than necessary.

"You moron. She's trying to help you when she needs help herself. You're not the only one hurt. Be nice." Joshua's voice was harsher in his ear than it ever had been before.

"I'm sorry." He meant it. She nodded slowly, but refused to meet his eyes. Brent closed his eyes and allowed Carter to help support him. It wasn't until he heard Alli talking about sand and petals that he opened his eyes. He told her to read out loud the directions word for word.

"Chew a single petal within ten seconds of picking and rub about a teaspoon of the top layer of the sand over the wound openings." As she read the instructions, Brent slumped against Carter. This was so unfair. Because of this, he would lose another month, and no matter how hopeless his case already was, it still felt like a punch in the gut.

133

"Anything else?" He had only injured himself this bad once before, and there had been a note from the enchantress that had explained why he had to do what he did. Apparently, at a certain point, his body couldn't heal itself without magic. The rose was basically the most magical thing in this place, and could therefore heal him. Of course, the downside to allowing him to live meant that it also took away from the time he had to break the curse.

"There a note at the bottom." Nice to know the enchantress cared about him. "'Sorry about the dosage. There was too much muscle damage. Plus those broken ribs didn't help. Don't worry too much.' There's some symbol at the bottom, but no name." Brent already knew the symbol was the enchantress' way of a signature, and broken ribs would explain the extreme pain he felt.

Nevertheless, he had to do what the instructions said. He began to do the best he could to sit up completely with the help of Carter.

"Stay still! You could..." Brent cut Alli's words off as Joshua stopped her from pushing him back down. He was slightly surprised that she still cared about what might happen to him, even if she didn't know what he needed.

"If I don't get to my room, I may never be able to use my arm properly ever again." He left out the part where he would most likely die of blood loss and shock.

Joshua loosely tied the thin towel around the wound and helped him stand up, along with

134

Carter. Brent had to grit his teeth in order to not shout at the pain. It felt worse now than it did before. His vision went completely black for a moment as he took a couple steps.

When they reached his bedroom door, Brent waited for Joshua and Carter to help him up the stairs, but then remembered they couldn't as Joshua slammed a hand against an invisible barrier. Brent groaned, realizing what this meant.

"What? Is something wrong?" Alli. Of course she could get past the barrier.

"Carter and I can't go into Brent's room." Brent didn't hear what else he said, but it didn't matter.

"Guys. Can we please talk a little less?" Brent knew his voice sounded strained, but he needed help.

"Help him." Carter didn't wait for any more pleasantries and practically dumped Brent on top of Alli, shoving them both toward the steps. Words couldn't express how much Brent wanted to hit Carter right about then. The force of his push almost took down both him and Alli in one blow. Oh, Lord give him the patience...

Alli was practically holding him up.

"Really?" He was honestly surprised somewhere deep in his mind at the anger in her voice, but there was too much pain to stay focused.

As Alli helped him up the stairs, Brent found himself immensely grateful for her assistance. Not that he would ever tell her that.

At the top of the stairs, he had to point her to the correct door. When she couldn't open it, Brent had to roll his eyes.

"Look up." She finally got the door open.

And there it was. The rose still looked almost the same as it was when he had last been here. Dying. Four petals left. Four months to go. Time was almost up.

"Pick one of the good petals." It was just like last time. Brent barely registered Alli's response, only putting the petal in his mouth.

He tried to pinch some of the top of the soil, but his hands were shaking so badly, Alli needed to do it for him once more. The flower was fragile enough without him harming it farther.

"What do I do?" The sound of her voice brought him back to the present.

"You read the instructions. Take about a teaspoon of the topsoil and press it against each bullet hole." Brent realized how shaky he sounded. The pain he felt must have seemed obvious to her. He noticed she wasn't moving. "Just do it."

He pulled back from her support and used the wall to sit down. He knew he needed to be sitting for what came next. When Alli came over and undid the cloth covering his wound, he braced himself as she pressed the topsoil against the bullet hole. Pain.

"Harder." Part of him could hardly believe that he had just told her to press harder. It would only cause more pain. He could feel the tiny grains of magic working its way into his bloodstream. It felt like someone was scrubbing the wound with sandpaper.

He had to remind her to do the other side. She applied even more pressure this time. Oh God, it hurt so bad. Still the pressure continued. Brent was gritting his teeth when the pain suddenly stopped. It was over. It was a strange sensation, going from pain to no pain. The tension left his muscles and he let out the breath he had been holding.

"Okay." Brent spoke quietly to Ali, although to his own ears, the words were almost deafening in the silence of the room. He looked over at her as she pulled away. Her hands were covered in his blood and she was white as death.

While she sat down, he carefully rolled his shoulder around, testing it out. Yep. It was healed. No more pain. He took the bloody towels lying on the ground and began to clean the red off his own body. He had a new scar to add to his growing collection. Part of him wondered if that was supposed to be symbolic of something. The other part of him really hoped not.

Brent could hear Alli's breath speeding up behind him. It sounded similar to when she had had the panic attack in the dining area. He turned to face her, just in time to catch her looking up at him. He was surprised at the intensity of angst and distress in her eyes. For a moment, she was frozen, before she buried her head in her arms. He, to his own astonishment, knelt next to her and pulled her trembling body into his arms. Her tears came harder and she leaned against him.

137

As he held the girl he had hated in high school two years back, Brent wondered if there was something he was missing. The Alli he saw now was very different from the one he had once known. Something about her had changed.

The thought struck him that it wasn't her who had changed, but him. He brushed the thought aside. Now was not the time for asking philosophical questions.

When Alli's tears had faded into silence, Brent looked down at her. She was completely asleep in his arms. He carefully picked her up and carried her out of the room. He made sure that the door shut behind him before he made his way out of his room and into the hallway.

As soon as he stepped into the hallway, Joshua and Carter jumped to their feet, ready to ask questions. Brent shook his head and a small half smile at the sight of them. They looked like their eyes were about to fall out of their heads.

Brent carried her to the medical room and carefully laid her down on the table. He could feel Joshua and Carter's gaze on his back as he grabbed a clean towel and got it wet, but he ignored them. He used the cloth to remove all blood from her hands and face. In the moonlight, she looked pale as death, and he found that that thought scared him to some extent.

When he had done the best he could to remove the blood, he just stared at her bruises. There was one large one on her right cheek and several lined her arms. Anger filled him. No matter

138

how much Alli had annoyed him in the past, she didn't deserve this type of treatment. He sucked in a breath and realized how tired he was.

Brent gathered her back into his arms and passed Joshua and Carter once more in the hallway as he carried Alli to her room. She seemed so light in his arms; it was a miracle that she had managed to support him at all. When he made it to her living room, he wondered if he would be able to go into her bedroom. Usually, there was a barrier there that would stop him. Before he could figure out what to do, he felt a strong tug at his arms. He felt Alli being pulled away from him, forcing him to let go of her.

She didn't fall and hit the ground. Her body stayed suspended in midair. Brent could only watch in amazement as she was pulled through the air until she settled down on top of her bed. That was definitely a first.

Maybe the magic really was changing. Brent rubbed his face tiredly, before finally turning to leave. Alli was safe. There was no point in staying. Before he could leave, the giant mural she had painted caught his eye. He stared at it for a long time before he realized what was different. The sun that was previously there was gone. In its place was the moon. The sky around it was dotted with millions of stars.

Brent slowly shook his head in amazement. What other changes would Alli bring?

Chapter 10

I found myself surrounded by darkness. The one pinpoint of light was a golden orb that consisted of a small grains of golden sand. There was nothing else. I looked around the darkness, hoping for an explanation.

"Keep watching." The soft voice of a young woman came from somewhere. I glanced around nervously before turning back to the golden orb. There was now a rose. It was just stem right now, but it was in the same glass pot I had seen before. The rose had yet to open.

Suddenly, the orb pulsed and time began to fly by. The green over the bud peeled down, revealing a small red flower about to bloom. The bud blossomed into a full rose. Time paused for a moment and I smiled slightly at the sight. It looked magical.

All of a sudden, time picked back up again. One by one, each petal disintegrated into small pieces that joined the golden orb above it. Even though the light grew stronger, the darkness around me grew denser and heavier. A sense of pain and dread replaced the once-peaceful atmosphere. Panic filled me when there were only three petals left on the *withering stem. Two petals. One. The flower was gone. All that was left was a small withered stem. The orb then dispersed with nothing to sustain it. The light vanished as a horrible cry filled the darkness.*

It echoed with pain and loneliness.

~*~

The sunlight blinded me as I sat up with a slight gasp, eyes wide open. I was in bed, covers crumpled around me. My clothes from yesterday were still on, splotches of dirt and what looked like blood stained them. I shakily got out of the bed and stumbled into the bathroom to look into the mirror.

I looked like I had been through a hurricane. The first thing I noticed was the dark bruise on my cheek. I did my best to not look at it, but my eyes kept coming back to it. There were bags under my eyes and I looked paler than usual. There wasn't any sign of any blood on my face though, even though I knew it had been there last night. I carefully touched the side of my head, finding two swollen knots. I quickly pulled my fingertips away.

As I got ready to shower, I came across the bruises on my arms. There was no doubt in my mind that what had happened last night was real. And if that was real, then the rose had to be as well.

After I showered and changed, I headed down to the medical room. I had forgotten about the cut in my palm and I probably needed to make sure that I didn't need anything for my other cuts and bruises. I considered getting Brent to come and help me, but I wasn't sure that I wanted to see him yet.

Sunlight made the medical room seem so bright, I could almost imagine that I was outside. When I took off the bandage, I found to my relief that the cut was healed for the most part. I wouldn't need a new bandage after all. All that was left was a bright red line that ran from the bottom of my hand to the base of my pinkie. It was a little sore, but after last night, that didn't matter very much. If there was a way to do anything for my bruises, the room didn't provide it. I guess I would have to just wait it out.

I made my way slowly to the dining area. It was very quiet and empty when I walking in the room. A moment later, the loud chiming sounded, and I realized it was lunchtime. No wonder I was so hungry!

I heard footsteps on the stairs behind me and turned to see a very sleep-deprived Brent. There were dark shadows under his eyes to attest to his lack of rest. He paused for a moment when he saw me, but his usual facade was broken by a large yawn. I smiled slightly at the sight, but that quickly faded into uncertainty. I looked at the floor.

"Thank you."

"You're welcome." An awkward silence filled the air before Brent let out a large breath. "Look." I made eye contact at his words. "-about yesterday. I- I'm sorry."

I didn't know how to exactly respond. I hadn't been expecting an apology, much less a sincere one.

143

"I-" I hesitated. "It's alright." For now. Another awkward pause. "Sorry for missing breakfast." I motioned to the food on the chairs.

"It's fine." Another unexpected answer.

"No one came to it." I turned to see Joshua walk in. I wondered how much he had heard of our conversation. He was shortly followed into the room by Carter, who picked up on the conversation quickly.

"Yeah. After a night like last night, everyone slept in."

Everyone gravitated towards the food. I joined them, but didn't make any moves to start eating, even though I was starving.

"What happened last night exactly?" At my words, all movement came to a halt. Brent stopped with a bite halfway into his mouth. I took the moment to continue. "You were shot and there was blood everywhere. But the rose and the sand-" I cut myself off, unsure of how to proceed. "I know now that there is magic in this place, but what exactly is going on here?" I felt almost like I was pleading for someone to speak.

"The magic-" Brent was obviously struggling to speak and he put down the plate of food, clasping his hands together. "I-I need that magic to heal and-" He broke off again. He seemed to struggle for words again before he finally gave up and stood up quickly and exited at a fast pace.

I stared after him for a bit before looking down. Was it really too much to ask? Was he hiding something?

144

"You know," Joshua broke the silence. "he wasn't always like this. Times have changed him a great deal." I stared at him wondering what exactly his words meant. "I remember him laughing and joking around." I couldn't believe what I was hearing. Brent laughing? "But not anymore." Joshua let out a small sigh and finished his food quickly before standing up and giving me one last look. "Try not to judge him immediately. If it is possible, show him how to enjoy life again." He left the fire, but paused briefly at his doorway. "Before it's too late."

It took a moment for me to realize that my question hadn't really been answered.

~*~

Brent was outside.

In the rush of everything that had happened last night, he hadn't realized where he had been. He had gone past the boundary. He couldn't anymore. He'd tested that. But now that he thought about it, he couldn't believe what he had done.

Alli. It had to be because of her. He didn't know whether to laugh or scream at the unfairness of it.

Eventually, he ended up on the edge of the cliff as usual. He stared out at the sea. He felt frustrated at himself that he hadn't been able to answer Alli's question. She really did make his life more difficult and complicated.

He knew that she deserved to have an answer. But how would he explain to her that she was supposed to fall in love with HIM, a guy so scarred that the sight of him had made her shrink

145

away in fear. On top of that, she hated the boy he used to be. It was an impossible situation.

Brent let out a small laugh of disbelief. Why did it have to be her? He rubbed his face tiredly. Under his fingers, he could feel the ditches left in his face by the scars.

He remembered the first time he had felt them. It was right after he had woken up in this place the first night. His body had felt full of fire. Just to breath had hurt. Eventually, the pain had faded, and he had sat up to see his body for what seemed to be the first time. It was almost like he was a billboard for scars. If he were in a freak show, he would most likely be one of the main attractions. The sight of his reflection had caused even him to jump back. At first, he couldn't stop staring at the change on his body, but now he didn't look in the mirror anymore if he could help it.

Brent had dropped the name 'Mark' then and there. The name hadn't felt like his anymore. Brent had been his middle name, and he had kept it from the first day.

It seemed so long ago now.

~*~

Late that night, I found myself on the cliffs outside. Call me stupid for going back outside so soon after almost being killed. Heck, I was still sore. You'd think that would be an appropriate reminder. I stared out at the town lights in the distance. The full moon shone bright against my skin, and a light breeze toyed with the tips of my hair, making them dance.

Brent was hiding something from me. It was something that had obviously changed him into who he is now. It didn't make complete sense. What had changed him, and how had he changed?

I leaned back on the grass beneath me and gazed at the stars. I could see them more clearly here than I could from my real home. Home. I wondered how Mom and Dan were. I had no way of knowing how they were now doing. I needed to know if Joshua and Carter had kept their end of the deal. I had kept my part so far, even though I had run away, or at least tried to run away. I still didn't know why the men wanted me here. It probably had to do with the whole magic thing. But how? The longer I thought about it, the more nothing made sense.

From behind me, the sound of soft footsteps registered. I scrambled into a half-sitting position before I realized it was just Brent. I knew he wasn't here to hurt me, so I laid back down on the cool ground. Out of the corner of my eye, I watched as Brent sat down next to me.

"Is there a reason that you're outside?" Brent's voice cut softly through the silence. I shrugged a little. "Do you really think it's wise to be here right now?"

"No." I already knew what he was saying was true, but I still felt silly as he pointed it out.

"So why are you here?"

"I don't know." I sat up and looked at him. "How did you know I was here?"

"I saw you come outside."

147

"Oh." He had been outside this whole time. A silence reigned. I bit my lip, wondering if he would get angry again if I asked him my question. "Why am I here?" I hated the way my voice came out sounding pitifully small. "Does the reason have something to do with the magic?" Brent looked at me for a while without responding.

"Yes." He didn't say anything else, even though I waited. I tried a different approach.

"Is my family alright?"

"Yes." This time his response was immediate.

"How do you know?"

"I've made sure to check in on them about once a week. They are fine. Your mom is very...active." I felt like crying and laughing at the same time. That sounded like Mom. Before she had gotten sick, she had more energy than the whole family put together daily. Apparently, she had gotten that energy back. A thought struck me.

"Are they still living in the same house? Small, white, almost no yard?" Brent looked thoughtful.

"Yes. I believe so. Is there a rundown park across the street?" I sighed with relief.

"That's the house." I thought a moment longer. "Is there a man there? Short and slightly potbellied? He has a bit of a temper."

"No." Brent shook his head. "Should there be?" I bit my lip, wondering how much I wanted Brent to know about my family.

148

"No. He shouldn't be." I said slowly. "My-my father isn't the kindest of men, and, you see, I just found out that he-well, he's on the run. The police are looking for him, and I just want him to stay away from Mom and Dan."

"Dan's your brother?" I nodded, looking out at the sea. After a long silence, I turned back to him.

"Why did you come after me? Wh-Why would you risk your life for a girl you barely know? Why would you care about what happened to someone like me?" Brent returned my gaze.

"I came after you because you were in trouble and would have died, I risked my life because it was the only way to save you, and I cared because I'm not inhumane." Not inhumane. That last part seemed to fill my ears like it was an accusation. I looked away.

Silence filled the night air, and I suddenly felt cold. When Brent stood up, I followed his lead. We both headed inside in a heavy silence. Somehow, I felt even worse than before.

Before I could disappear into my room, Brent's voice stopped me.

"You might want to avoid going outside for a little bit, especially after dark." I just nodded, knowing he would most likely be able to see me.

When I went to my room, I just sat on my bed. Why did I feel so bad? Brent's words kept ringing in my ears. It took a long time to fall asleep that night. Even then, the words resounded in my dreams.

~*~

"...not inhumane." Even as the words left Brent's mouth, he doubted himself. Alli looked away from him, so he couldn't tell what she was thinking. She probably doubted him, too. He stood up when he saw her shiver, and she was quick to follow him inside.

"You might want to avoid going outside for a little bit, especially after dark." Brent could barely make out her nod of acceptance. When she disappeared into her room, he made his way back outside.

The night air helped clear his thoughts.

Alli wasn't afraid of him anymore.

Part of him was thrilled at that notion, but another part of him detested her. She had caused so much trouble and pain already. Thanks to her, he had one less month to live free. Not that it would have made a difference to the end result.

To take the enchantress' advice or not. That was the question.

~*~

Part of me wondered if mealtimes were destined to be the most awkward parts of the day. Over breakfast, Carter was missing. Joshua told me that he had a job out in the city. After that, silence fell on us. I finished relatively quickly, leaving the room as soon as I could.

I went down to the library to find something to do. There was nothing different from the last time I had been here. There were still books piled everywhere in precarious stacks and, if anything, there were even more books than before. I wandered deeper into the precarious stacks of books, every once in a while taking note of the topics of the books. To my surprise, I reached a point where more diverse genres were suddenly appearing. I thought that I had made a thorough search before. Interesting.

I began to see books by people like Shakespeare mixed with Jane Austen. As I searched the bookshelves, the topics grew more varied, and I found myself sorting through them. Amongst the books, I lost all sense of time. They made me feel safe.

I wondered if there would be a book somewhere that could explain the magic of this place. Surely, there had to be something. I sighed and let out a huff of air. There was no way that I would be able to keep track of anything. There was no organization.

I looked on the side of the bookshelves and saw that there were small, empty, metal frames used for labeling. Well, now I knew a way to organize. I ran quickly to my room and grabbed some paper and a pen before bringing it back to the library. I quickly began to divide up the bookshelves, working as fast as I could. It was as though more and more shelves just kept appearing the longer I worked. How long I labored, I don't know.

I was shaken out of my work mode when the loud ringing of the dinner bell penetrated the library walls. It took several seconds for it to register that it was dinner time, not lunch. Whoops.

I quickly put down the volumes in my arms and made my way to the entrance, wondering if I would be in trouble for the skipped meal. I opened the door, only for it to bounce back sharply with force as it slammed into someone. I carefully opened the door again and peeked around the wood to see Carter standing there, holding his nose. I chose to ignore the muffled curses he was muttering under his breath.

"Oh....Sorry." I winced. That had to have hurt. At the sound of my voice, Carter looked up, looking surprised and perhaps a bit angry.

"Where have you been?" I looked at him funnily. Shouldn't it be obvious?

"I was in the library." I stuck a thumb behind me, making it even more obvious for him.

"All day?" I nodded slowly.

"Yeah." Carter let out a huff of air, holding his nose with one hand.

"Right." He motioned towards the dining hall with his head. "Come on." I followed him to dinner, still slightly confused.

When I got to the room, Brent and Joshua were already there. When I entered, both stopped eating and stared at me. I wondered it there was something on my face, but there was nothing there when I checked.

"Where have you been?" "Is there something wrong?" Brent spoke at the same time as me, and I flushed slightly.

"I was in the library." I bit my lip slightly. "Sorry. I didn't hear the lunch bell and just sort of lost track of time..." I slowly made my way to my seat. Brent shook his head slightly as if he couldn't believe me.

"What were you doing there?" I had to be honest, I was surprised that Brent cared enough to ask. He sounded almost...relieved as he spoke.

"Well, you could say that I'm organizing it. But I haven't gotten far."

"Why are you organizing the library?" I set down the bite of food I was about to take.

"I wasn't exactly planning to...It just kind of happened. I was looking for a book that might tell me something about this place." I could tell that Brent was interested now. Strange.

"Did you find what you were looking for?"

"No. Not yet." Disappointment flickered across Brent's face. "But I've only just started. There's still a long way to go." Brent's eyes danced through several emotions, even though his face was unmoving. I could see excitement there, and almost smiled when he caught my observing look and forced his face to the fire. He wasn't hiding very well.

Throughout the rest of the meal, I allowed small smiles to slip onto my mouth as Brent began to look more and more impatient. When he finally left the dining room, I smiled, amused. This Brent was different from before, and I wondered what had caused that change. I was about to leave when I noticed the look that Joshua and Carter were giving me. The smile slipped from my face, and I frowned slightly before heading up the stairs. They looked as if they knew something that I didn't. I hated not knowing things.

Once I was just out of their sight, I paused, realizing they had begun to talk. Snippets of the conversation floated up to me.

"...she could...don't you think?" I couldn't hear the murmured reply.

"But...hope....maybe?" There wasn't any more sounds after that, and I moved on, now more confused than ever as I made my way to my room.

Was there something that I was supposed to do? If so, then what? I felt like I was being tested.

Chapter 11

I spent the next two days alone and in relative peace. I was used to being by myself, but after two days of only me and the books, I was starting to feel lonely. Not to mention that I had barely made headway in the whole organizing the library business. I was beginning to question whether or not I should keep it up.

Sometime close to dinner on the second day, I found myself lying on one of the cushioned chairs, eyes closed, feet dangling over the side. I heard the library door open and tilted my head back farther to see who it was. Joshua. I closed my eyes and relaxed again.

I heard his footsteps pause for a moment and then a quiet laugh.

"I see you weren't kidding when you said there was still a long way to go." I twisted in the chair to see him better. He really was right. There were books everywhere. It was as if some book monster had thrown up books everywhere.

Joshua attempted to move farther into the library, only to knock over several stacks of theology books. I couldn't help but laugh at his lack of coordination. Finding some stored energy, I got up and helped him put the books back into their respective piles.

"Do you know where all of these books came from?"

"Not a clue." I glanced at him, trying to figure out if he was just trying to be difficult.

"Do you mean that you don't know where they came from or that you can't tell me?" Joshua paused what he was doing and looked at me.

"I guess that depends on how you look at it." And I guess that answered that. After a few more pitiful attempts to ask him questions, I gathered that he didn't really want to answer anything that related to him in any way. Several more awkward moments followed, until the dinner bell signaled.

Joshua left immediately, but I waited a few more seconds to gather myself before following.

Dinner was just underway when I had a sudden idea.

"Brent?" I waited for him to look at me. "Does the library have an index book or a list of all the books there?" Brent looked like he was trying to remember.

"I believe there used to be one, but I haven't seen it for over a year." I bit my lip slightly, thinking aloud.

"If I could find that, it should be easier to divide the library up and find what I'm looking for." I took a couple more bites of food before I spoke again. "H-have you read all of the books there?" I didn't think so, but there was always a chance, and it would explain all of the books everywhere. After all, he seemed to have quite a bit of time.

Brent hesitated.

"Let's just say that I have a lot of time to kill." He gave me a look that didn't leave room for conversation.

"Right...Well, do you have an idea where the index should be?" Brent looked back at me again.

"Try the very back. There's a pedestal where it used to be."

"Gotcha." I set my mostly empty plate down. "Now I just have to find the back of the library."

~*~

About two hours later, I was thumbing the pages of a very heavy and a very thick book. There weren't very many book names or authors per page, but the index also included book genres, time period the book was written in, and small, sentence summaries. It was fairly detailed. So far, I hadn't recognized a single book or author. I read a lot, so I was slightly surprised at this fact.

I had wasted so much time trying to find the Index that I was feeling a little edgy. That, accompanied with the fact that the book was really heavy, I chose to remain on the floor. About an hour passed before I realized how uncomfortable the floor was. The lower half of my body was starting to go numb from sitting for so long. I shoved the giant book off of my lap and stood up, stretching. I picked the index up with a grunt and began to make my way to a better place to sit.

I had to watch where I was going so much that I almost ended up lost on my way to the front of the library. Eventually, I made my way to the entrance and collapsed into one of the sitting chairs. Just as I began to open the index once more, everything went black.

My breath caught in my throat until I realized that it must have been lights out time.

"Oh no." I let out a quiet groan in the darkness. My eyes began to adjust, but it was no use. There was absolutely no way I would be able to see anything without a source of light. I let the index drop off my lap as I carefully stood up, suddenly dreadfully aware of how quiet everything seemed. There wasn't a sound to be heard, except for my slightly erratic breathing.

Mentally assuring myself that I was safe, I carefully began to make my way through the inky black, hoping not to run into anything. Every other step or so, my foot would slam into books, and several times, loud thumps resounded as the massive volumes fell off of their respective stacks. Of course, my luck never holds out. I soon tripped over a small stack of books, causing me to fall into several larger stacks, setting off a small landslide of books and a burst of pain in my right ankle. I let out a loud yelp in the darkness and gritted my teeth. That. Hurt. A lot.

I stayed still for several moments, sucking in several deep breaths before slowly sitting up again. I tried to move my foot, but soon stopped when another sharp sting made me yelp again. I carefully ran the tips of my fingers over the quickly swelling spot. There was no way that I would be able to go anywhere on that.

I moved my arms around me until they hit one of the sitting chairs. I did my best to shift my body nearer and lean against it. I squeezed my eyes shut and tried to focus on something besides my ankle. It didn't work too well. My breathing seemed very loud once more. I immediately began to monitor it so that I wouldn't start having a panic attack.

I remained in that position for a little longer before a slight screeching sound came from somewhere on my left. I opened my eyes and startled at the sound, cringing in pain at the movement.

A faint light shone in the darkness, and soon I could make out Brent coming down the steps, holding a lit torch.

"Oh." I let out a sigh of relief at the sight of him. "Thank goodness." I let out a strained laugh at my jumpiness.

"What are you doing?" Brent tried to piece together the information as he maneuvered around several stacks of books. As he got closer, he must have seen the strained look on my face. "Did something happen? What's wrong?"

I was surprised to detect concern in his voice as he knelt next to me on the floor.

"I-ah-I got caught here after lights out and kind of..." I gestured towards my foot. "I either sprained or broke my ankle. Probably a sprain." I let out another slightly strained laugh before hissing in pain as Brent gently touched the swollen ankle. I looked at him just in time to see him roll his eyes. I almost laughed when I realized that he more exasperated than angry at the fact that I had managed to get into trouble again.

"Can you stand?" I bit my lower lip and slowly stood up on my left foot. I leaned shakily against the chair behind me for support.

"Yes." My answer was so obvious I didn't even have to look at him to know Brent was rolling his eyes again. I carefully began to put weight on my right foot, but no sooner had I done so when lightning shot up my leg and I collapsed. I let out a loud gasp and blinked back a few tears. It took a moment to recover, and I soon realized that I wasn't on the ground.

I had both arms around Brent's shoulder, while he held me up with one arm and the torch in the other. I don't know how he managed it. Just as I began to realize how strange I felt being so close to him, he shoved the torch into one of my hands. Before I could speak, he had hooked his other arm under my knees, and I let out another yelp as he picked me up.

"I--you--okay." I shut up when he rolled his eyes for the third time and gave me a look that obviously said: *Do you* want *help?*

I found myself very glad that he was carrying me. It was much more comfortable than the floor. Brent carried me out of the library and straight to the medical room. He sat me down on the table before taking away the torch and putting it in a metal holder inside the room. It wasn't until then that I realized how warm his arms had been.

Meanwhile, Brent had taken a splint and some cold packs out of the cupboard. I began to gingerly remove my shoe, wincing at how swollen my ankle now was as I peeled back my sock. Brent cracked and shook the ice packs to get them cold before passing them to me.

"Ow." I hissed again at the cold sensation. I wanted to throw the ice pack across the room.

"How did you manage to get caught in the dark again?" Brent was leaning against one of the counters opposite of me with his arms loosely crossed. I shrugged, secretly glad for the distraction.

"I guess I just got distracted...again." I realized that I got distracted very often. "I guess it would help if I had a watch." I thought for a moment, frowning slightly. "I think I have one somewhere..." I shrugged again, giving up on the subject for the time being. There was a lull in the conversation.

"Where did you get that?" I nodded towards the torch on the wall.

"It's for emergencies." I let him elaborate. "I heard some loud crashes and *someone* yelling, so I decided to investigate." Brent shifted slightly, his face falling into the moonlight. He was looking at me with almost no expression, as if he didn't want me to find something out.

We both fell quiet and a heavy silence reigned. I checked my ankle, looking for something

161

to do, and to my surprise, some of the swelling had already gone down. That was a first. It took me a moment to remember the magic. I guess that would explain it.

"Here." Brent passed me the splint, which he had undone. I clenched my teeth as I pulled it on, even though I couldn't feel anything for the most part. I tightened the straps, and almost felt an immediate relief from pain. If that was because of magic, then I was all for it.

"You wouldn't happen to have crutches, would you?" I looked at Brent hopefully, but he just shook his head.

"You should be able to walk."

I just looked at him.

"Try it."

I didn't like it, but I did what he said.

To my surprise, I found that I could stand on it with no problem. I tried to walk, but found that to still be uncomfortable enough not to continue.

"It should feel better by morning." *Should?* I looked at him as he came towards me. "I'll help you to your room."

The trip to my room that resulted was both painful and awkward to say the least as I leaned against Brent for support. We made it to my living room before he stopped at the entrance to my bedroom. He left me there and turned to leave, so I grabbed his arm to stop and thank him.

"You're welcome." He still said those words with a slight pause as though he hadn't expected any thanks. Again.

I contemplated whether or not I was desperate enough to attempt to go up the stairs. After much pondering, I found myself sleeping on the small couch in the living room instead. It saved me a lot of trouble

It was then that I decided that the couch didn't seem as hard as before.

Magic must truly be everywhere.

Chapter 12

I managed to get up earlier than usual in order to shower before breakfast. The sun was just coming in through the windows in streams of gold and pick when I made my way to the living room once more.

I remembered that my ankle was supposed to be hurting. Now that I thought about it, I realized that I still had the brace on. I wondered if it was a bad thing that I had just showered with it on. Whoops. I didn't have any idea how I had missed taking it off.

The fact that I didn't need crutches to walk surprised me to no end. The last time I had hurt my ankle like that, it was several days, at least, before I could walk on my own. And yet, here I was. Walking.

I started to leave my room, but a flash of light caught my eye from outside. I saw that it was the first glint of the sunlight on the ocean and spent the next several minutes staring at the sunrise. Both the one outside and the one in the mural. It still amazed me how similar the two scenes were. Eventually, I pulled myself away and made my way back to the library. The library was probably the only place that I could honestly say that I loved in this cliff home. As disorienting as it could be, I felt safer there than I did in most places.

As I made my way to the library, torches sprang to life as I passed them. By the time I got to the library entrance, the entire hallway behind me was more brightly lit than I had ever seen it before. It was almost enough to make the stone walls look warm and homey.

The torches in the library were already lit by the time I got there, which surprised me. I hadn't planned on someone already being here. Maybe if I got lucky, I wouldn't see anyone at all until breakfast.

There wasn't anyone at the first glance, so I began to make my way down the main aisle, stopping every once in a while to pick up a fallen stack of books. I was seriously pondering shoving them all onto the bookshelves before organizing.

At last, I came to the very back where the index pedestal stood. I stopped short of it when I noticed that the index was sitting on it. I never put it back last night, and yet there it was, open on its pedestal. I looked around again. Someone had to be here.

Out of the corner of my eye, I notice someone's shoe poking out from between one of the bookshelves. I quietly made my way over, and to my amazement, I saw Brent sitting on the ground, back to the side of a bookshelf, fast asleep.

I immediately felt as though I was intruding, but I didn't leave. He looked so relaxed; it was startlingly different from the way he usually held himself. His expression wasn't guarded. I began to slowly back away from him, and had just made it a couple feet when the breakfast bell rang loudly. The noise startled me, and I yelped, jumping and knocking over a stack of book. I backed away quickly, but I guess my ankle wasn't quite up to it yet and a small sharp pain flared in my ankle. I bent down to rub it, completely forgetting that Brent was literally right behind me.

"Allison?" At the sound of his voice, I jerked once more and twisted, still holding onto my ankle, which resulted in me falling back. In a situation much like when we first met, Brent lunged forward and caught me before I hit the ground.

"Hi." I tried to sound as though he wasn't keeping me from hitting the ground, but failed miserably. I sounded like I had been caught with my hand in the cookie jar. Brent gave me a small smirk and pulled me up. I grabbed hold of his arm to keep myself from toppling right back over with the leftover momentum. "Thanks." I gave a half-grin, half-grimace. Brent just gave me a grimace.

"What were you doing in here?" He stared at me with a strange look, and I contemplated telling him that I had drawn a moustache on his face.

"Well..." I drew out the word. "I was planning on coming here to read a little before breakfast, but when I saw you asleep, I, well, I tried to leave, but then the bell rang and I jumped, and

167

then the books spilled everywhere, and then-" Brent went ahead and cut off my rambling.

"Okay. I get it." Brent rubbed his face and stifled a yawn.

"Right."

"Yeah." Awkward silence.

"Right. Breakfast." I mumbled and turned to leave, tripping slightly on a stray book as I went. I saw Brent shake his head as he went to follow me and sighed quietly. I got that a lot.

Breakfast was the normal, silent affair, but I found that it didn't bother me much anymore. The silence was more welcoming now than the awkward tension, although I still wished that Joshua and Carter would talk more. Maybe they did whenever I wasn't there.

Joshua finished much quicker than normal before disappearing out the exit. I followed him with my eyes until he had disappeared from sight before looking at Brent and Carter.

"It's his turn to go into town." Carter gave me a very generic answer to my silent question. I nodded in acknowledgement, and we all fell quiet again.

As usual, I ended up leaving early to escape the ongoing cycle of silence. Once more, I went to the library and ended up on one of the giant chairs there. Almost as soon as I sat down, I heard a loud bang as someone opened the door to the library. Joshua was too quiet for that and he wasn't here, and Brent was...well, Brent, so that only left one person. Sure enough, Carter soon came into view.

He completely ignored my confused look and soon disappeared from view among the many bookshelves. I stared after him for a moment before getting up and following. I must say, in the time I've been here, I don't remember ever seeing him in the library.

I found him scanning the bookshelves.

"What are you doing?" At the sound of my voice, Carter looked up, seemingly embarrassed.

"Looking for a book." Oh? That's all? I thought you were looking for a new pet.

"What book?" I prompted.

"Shakespeare." Why would he be embarrassed about that?

"Okay...Ummm. I don't know exactly where it is, but I can help look if you want." It sounded more like a question when the words came out of my mouth, but Carter look immediately grateful. He then turned around and directly left the library.

"You're welcome." I mutter under my breath, astounded. I offer to help and he then leaves? Did he expect me to find the book on my own? Well, no way. I wasn't his servant.

I made my way back to the chairs up front and plopped back down. I didn't feel like doing any organizing, but I wasn't bored enough yet to search for Shakespeare. I shifted in the chair, trying to find a comfortable position. Among the many positions I tried, there was one of me upside down with my feet in the air and my hair just brushing the ground. I would have never even tried that position had I known that there was someone else in the room.

"What are you doing?" I let out a surprised yelp at the sound of Brent's voice coming from somewhere to my right. In my haste to sit up straight, I almost turned a complete somersault, barely catching myself before I hit the ground.

"You really shouldn't sneak up on people like that." I sounded a little breathless as I finally ended up sitting with my back to the chair. "I was...well..." I didn't know how to say anything without sounding like a complete idiot.

"Never mind." Brent saved me the trouble by stopping me. "I don't need to know." I smiled weakly and an awkward silence fell upon us. Brent finally had enough and eventually turned away to pick his way towards the back of the room, out of my sight. I inwardly grimaced at our lack of creativity to come up with anything conversation-worthy.

After sitting around lazily for a little longer, I dragged myself over to one of the bookshelves in order to begin sorting once more. I was in the process of pulling several books off of said bookshelf when I heard a loud crash from the back of the library, followed by several loud swears.

I dumped the books in my arms on the floor and made my way quickly toward the back, following the direction of the curses. I suddenly turned one of the corners and put a hand up to cover the smile on my mouth, but that did little to help. The sight in front of me caused a few giggles to escape before I could stop them.

170

At the sound of my laughter, Brent looked up from his place on the floor and scowled. Apparently there were some more chairs back here, because there was one on top of his legs, pinning him down. He might have been able to get out from under it, if not for the bookshelf stopping him. I could barely see Brent for all of the books piled around him.

"It's not funny." Brent tried to look serious under the pile of books, the chair, and the bookshelf, but it wasn't working very well. I took a little longer to observe Brent's situation.

"Yes, it is." I choked out before bursting into a fresh round of laughter. I settled down after a couple seconds, but when I saw the scowl on Brent's face grow deeper, I began to laugh again. "This is very funny, and you know it!" It was easier to be less scared of him when he was as trapped as he was. Brent's scowl disappeared and I noticed a hint of a small smile.

"Help me get the bookshelf off." I could tell Brent was having a hard time controlling himself, so I did my best to push the shelf off of him. He did what he could with his legs pinned, but eventually, the bookshelf was upright once more.

"And you think I'm accident prone." I grunted while we shoved the armchair upright. Brent didn't verbally reply as he finally got to his feet, but I had a feeling that he was rolling his eyes. Again. I sat down on the newly-righted armchair.

"Brent?" I leaned back and looked at him in the eyes.

171

"What?" He had begun to put up his guarded expression once more.

"Smile. It's not going to hurt." He gave some kind of grimace and I began to giggle. He wasn't very good at this. Brent rolled his eyes again and took a step back, only to immediately bang his head against the shelf I had just righted. He let out a hiss and glared at the offending shelf. I did my absolute best to not begin laughing again. It almost worked.

To distract myself, I began to pile up all of the book now lying on the ground. Out of the corner of my eye, I saw Brent smiling. It wasn't a grimace or even a half smile. It was a real smile. I didn't look at him, just in case he would stop smiling. It really did make him look a whole lot nicer.

Brent got down to help me and soon the books were back on the bookshelf in a not-so-organized chaos. I made sure we hadn't missed any on the books in the near vicinity, and to my surprise, my eyes fell on the exact book I wanted. Shakespeare.

"Hey." I pick the book up. Sure enough, it was a complete copy of the works of Shakespeare.

"What?" Brent wasn't smiling anymore, but he wasn't scowling either.

"Oh, nothing. Carter was actually here just before you were, looking for this book. He looked strangely embarrassed about looking for it." A strange expression crossed Brent's face, and I looked at him curiously.

"He was actually looking for that for me. I wanted to read the plays." I didn't know whether to laugh outright or just stare at Brent. I would have never guessed in a million years that Brent would be the kind of person to want to read Shakespeare for fun.

"Okay." I tried to make all of the shock and awe go out of my voice, but I could tell by Brent's grimace that I hadn't done it right. I tried again. "That's really neat!" I pretty much failed at that attempt as well. Both of us waited for a couple of seconds before standing up at some unspoken cue. "Where are you going?" I decided to switch the entire conversation away from Shakespeare.

"Outside." I wanted to go outside so much. Brent must have seen that, because in the next instant, he asked, "Do you want to come too?"

I would probably only embarrass myself if I spoke, so I settled for a quick nod and a smile. Both of us got up, and, at the last minute, I grabbed a few books that I had set aside for personal reading.

The outside clearing was just as, if not more beautiful than I remembered. It truly was something out of a story book, as though every tree, plant, flower had been arranged just so. There was a sense of comfort that I loved.

Brent settled himself down at the base of a large tree near the edge of the cliff with a familiarity that told me that he had come here before to read. I sat about ten feet away from him, a bit farther from the cliff edge. I must have started to read one of my books five times before my curiosity got the better of me.

"Have you read them before?" Brent looked up from his book at the sound of my voice.

"What?"

"Shakespeare's plays." I gestured at the book in his hand. "Have you read them?"

"I tried. It didn't work out too well." Something in common.

"Same here. I read Macbeth, but I'm afraid that I still don't understand it completely." It suddenly dawned on me that I was having a semi-normal conversation with Brent and I immediately felt self-conscious. I rubbed my head as I tried to recall the first few lines of the play. "When shall we three meet again..." I couldn't remember the rest.

"...in thunder, lightning, or in rain?[1]" Brent finished the first sentence, and I felt my face heat up when I realized that I had spoken those words out loud.

"You've read this before?" Brent shook his head.

"No. School play." Of course Brent had gone to school. That thought had just never crossed my mind.

"My school once did Macbeth too, but I didn't go to see it."

"Why?" I bit my lip and looked away. I could tell that Brent was actually trying to keep up a conversation with me, but I didn't like the memories that this particular story brought up.

"I was supposed to help manage costumes for the play, but I couldn't because of...family complications."

"Tell me about the play." He didn't seem to get that I didn't want to.

"Umm...well, it's just about the same as the play in the book." Maybe he would be satisfied.

"What happened?" Or not. He sounded almost as quiet as I did. I didn't know whether that was a good or bad sign.

"Well, you see...At my school, there was this boy, Mark, and we didn't exactly get along. He was...amazing really. Everyone loved him, but he was very proud and...mean. At least, he was to me, I don't know about other people, but..." I trailed off briefly, before starting again, but much more softly. "Anyway, the boy, Mark, was in one of the lead roles, and he noticed that I wasn't there. I don't know what he said, but I was...cornered the next day by some of his friends. Nothing bad happened, but..." I knew that it would be obvious to Brent what had happened, but I didn't feel like going into details. Detail didn't matter too much though; Brent got the gist of it.

"They hit you." His voice had a hollow ring to it.

"But...That was over two years ago. Mark left soon after that, so things haven't been too bad. There isn't much use dwelling in the past, now, is there?" I tried to sound a bit more cheerful, but Brent wasn't looking at me anymore. He was staring into space somewhere over the ocean. "Brent?" I hesitantly reached out a hand and touched his leg, as it was the closest limb to me.

175

He jolted at my touch, and I quickly pulled my hand back. His eyes looked full of frustration, sadness, and slight disbelief. "Are you okay?" I hadn't expected my story to affect him so much.

"Yes." In spite of the raging emotion in his eyes, his voice remained flat. "I'm fine."

"Are you angry at me?"

"No." He looked slightly surprised that I had asked that. "These friends of Mark's, do they still bother you?" I gave a partial smile.

"Very, very rarely." That answer didn't seem to satisfy him. "You don't need to worry about me. It's all in the past. Anyway, I'm here now aren't I? They can't reach me here." My words didn't help much.

"No. No, they can't." Brent stood up and left me in the clearing, leaving the book of plays behind.

Chapter 13

When Brent saw that Carter had come back from the library empty-handed, he rolled his eyes. He never could understand why Carter hated that place so much.

"Get your own Shakespeare." Carter mumbled as he walked past. Brent looked at him funny.

"What happened to you?" No answer. He had to do everything himself, didn't he?

Brent got up from the fire and made his way to the library. He was definitely not expecting to see Alli upside down on one of the chairs.

"What are you doing?" The words slipped out before he could stop them. It was quite entertaining to watch Alli's face when she was so startled. He had to hold back a laugh when she barely managed to catch herself from hitting the ground. She looked so embarrassed that he almost felt sorry for her.

"You really shouldn't sneak up on people like that." She remained on the floor, looking at him with wide eyes. He was glad to see that there wasn't fright in them, so much as surprise. "I was...well..." When she seemed to struggle to come up with an

177

answer, Brent just stopped her. She gave him an almost smile in return. Silence reigned. He hated silence, especially now, when there was only Joshua and Carter to talk to.

Right. He hadn't come to stand around. Brent headed to the back of the library. That's where he had last put the book. If only he could remember where exactly he had put it.

In the back of the library, to the right, there were a couple of armchairs. He enjoyed this spot much better than the chairs near the entrance to the library. Something about the way the spot was hidden appealed to him.

He sat on the arm of the chair to observe the shelf in front of him.

Then it happened. Brent had no idea how it managed to happen, but apparently it can be very disastrous when tilting a heavy armchair. The thing fell onto his legs, and trying to stay upright, he tried to use the shelf as support. Of course, his weight was enough to bring the entire thing down on top of him, trapping him even more. Brent barely had time to cover his face before a ton of books rained down on him.

He proceeded to exhaust his store of curses. Whoever said that words didn't hurt had obviously never had an entire bookshelf fall on top of them. They hurt. But so did the wooden shelf, pinning down the armchair, pinning down him.

When he heard soft laughter, he shoved aside several books until he could see the source.

From where he was on the floor, he could just barely see Alli trying to contain her laughter.

"It's not funny." He probably shouldn't have said anything. She moved, allowing him to see her face better.

"Yes, it is." She began to laugh again. He scowled deeper, but it didn't help. He must have looked like quite a spectacle in order for her to laugh so freely. "It's very funny and you know it!" That was the problem. He thought that it was funny, but he wasn't about to tell her that. Nevertheless, his scowl disappeared and he found himself fighting to not smile.

"Help me get the bookshelf off." He began to use his hands to shove aside as many of the books as he could manage. Thankfully, she seemed to be able to compose herself enough to begin to lift the shelf up. In spite of wanting to smile, the weight on his legs really did hurt. He had to hold back a groan when the weight of the bookshelf finally disappeared. He was worried for a moment that the shelf would be too much for Alli to support and it might fall back down, but, thankfully, Alli managed to right it without much trouble.

With that weight off of him, he could finally get out from under that infernal armchair.

"And you think I'm accident prone." He could clearly hear Alli muttering under her breath and almost laughed. He did settle for an eye roll, and he had a feeling she knew that he was doing so. He slowly got to his feet, trying to regain the feeling in his legs once more. Pins and needles filled them.

"Brent?" Brent looked up at the sound of Alli's voice. She was sitting on the armchair.

"What?"

"Smile. It's not going to hurt." He must have been scowling. He did his best to smile, but didn't put much effort into it, causing it to come out more like a grimace. She giggled at him. She wasn't helping. He took a step away and promptly banged his head against the shelf behind him. He must have been standing closer to it than he had originally thought. He sucked in a quick breath. That really hurt. He glared at the shelf.

When he turned back to Alli, he saw that she was picking up several books from the floor. She was biting her lip to keep from smiling at him. He wondered what was causing her good mood. She looked like she was trying so hard to not smile that he had to smile. If she looked up right at that moment, she would definitely catch him in the act. He waited until he could control himself before he got down on his knees to help her.

Brent was just placing a book on the shelf when he heard Alli.

"Hey." He looked at her.

"What?"

"Oh, nothing. Carter was actually here just before you were, looking for this book. He looked strangely embarrassed about looking for it." Oh. That. Brent suddenly understood why Carter had come back empty-handed and embarrassed.

"He was actually looking for that for me. I wanted to read the plays."

"Okay." Brent wished he could take back his words. Alli was staring at him with a slightly bemused look that showed her disbelief in him. "That's really neat!" If she was trying to make him feel better, it wasn't working.

Before things could get to awkward, Brent stood up. He wasn't expecting Alli to stand up with him. He wondered if she was mimicking him.

"Where are you going?"

"Outside." The moment he said that, a wistful expression crossed her face. Should he ask her to come? Would she want to come if it meant being with him? "Do you want to come too?" She flashed him a small, but genuine smile that told him 'yes'. A small part of him did a fist pump at her acceptance. She walked beside him as they left the library, only slowing down to grab some books for herself.

Brent's favorite place was the clearing outside, and judging from the look on Alli's face, she agreed. He found himself reclining against the same tree where he first watched Alli arrive at the beginning of the summer. He opened the book in his hands and began to flip to the beginning of a random play.

"Have you read them before?" The sound of Alli's voice startled Brent from his thoughts, and he looked up to see her watching him, chin perched on her knees and her books on the ground next to her, unopened.

"What?" He acted as though he hadn't heard her so that he could gather his thoughts.

181

"Shakespeare's plays." She pointed vaguely at the book in his lap. "Have you read them before?"

"I tried. It didn't work out too well." Alli looked strangely relieved.

"Same here. I read Macbeth, but I'm afraid that I still don't understand it completely." That explained it. She looked down a second later, looking flustered as she ran a hand through her hair. She mumbled part of the first line.

"...in thunder, lightning, or rain?[1]" He automatically recited the rest of the sentence. Alli jerked up her head, bright red. He almost smiled at the look of embarrassment on her face. Just almost.

"You've read this before?" Brent leaned back a bit against the tree trunk and shook his head.

"No. School play." She got that contemplative look on her face again.

"My school once did Macbeth too, but I didn't go to see it."

"Why?" Now that she had brought it up, he remembered that she was supposed to be there. She had missed the main event, even though they had needed her there. Alli averted her eyes, suddenly seeming smaller.

"I was supposed to help manage costumes for the play, but I couldn't because of...family complications." She didn't elaborate any further, but still Brent wondered. She had been back at school the next day, but he didn't remember much else.

"Tell me about the play."

"Umm...Well, it's just about the same as the play in the book." She seemed to be dancing around something.

"What happened?" Brent spoke softer, wondering if it had to do with her father. She was silent for a long time before she continued.

"Well, you see...At my school, there was this boy, Mark, and we didn't exactly get along. He was..." Oh. He couldn't remember what he had done. She sounded almost frightened. "...amazing really. Everyone loved him, but he was very proud and...mean." Brent felt his expression closing off. Her words rang true and hard. "At least, he was to me, I don't know about other people, but..." Others? Now that he thought about it, there probably were. It had been so long ago. "Anyway, the boy, Mark, was in one of the lead roles of the play and he noticed that I wasn't there. I don't know what he said, but I was...cornered the next day by some of his friends. Nothing bad happened, but..." Cornered. He hadn't known that.

"They hit you." Alli refused to meet his eye, and for a while, there was silence.

"But...That was over two years ago. Mark left soon after that, so things haven't been too bad since. There isn't much use dwelling in the past, now, is there?" If she was trying to lighten the mood, it wasn't working. He was really starting to doubt that he knew everything that had caused Alli to hate him so much in school. He was starting to see that her experiences were much grimmer than he originally thought.

He felt a hand on his leg and jerked, turning to see Alli pulling away from him, startled.

"Are you okay?" The irony that she was asking him that question was not lost on him.

"Yes. I'm fine." Of course not.

"Are you angry at me?" She thought he was mad at her? No way. Especially not after hearing her side of the story. He wondered how many times she had thought that question when he was around.

"No." He paused. "These friends of Mark's, do they still bother you?" Please say no.

"Very, very rarely." He couldn't believe it. What had he started? "You don't need to worry about me. It's all in the past. Anyway, I'm here now aren't I? They can't reach me here."

"No. No, they can't." Brent got off of the floor and made straight for the portal. He needed to be away from her. She always brought his emotions just close enough to the surface that he might lose control, and he didn't want that. He escaped to his room for a couple of hours, until he knew Alli wouldn't be outside anymore, and then he returned.

Outside, the wind was now blowing hard, and he could see distant, ominous clouds out over the sea. Brent let himself fall to his knees near the cliff edge. In his mind, he began to play back all of the scenes he could remember from two years back that had involved him and Alli. After several moments, Brent came to the realization that he couldn't even remember seeing her smile while they were both in school.

"Yes. She never did smile, did she?" Brent jerked, startled.

"Back so soon?" He did his best to sound as though he didn't care, but it came out more angry than he planned.

"Yes." The enchantress was sitting with her back against the tree, casually watching the storm growing over the sea. He wondered if she knew that he had asked a rhetorical question. "Have you changed your mind about Alli yet?" He didn't answer her for a long time. When he did, he changed the topic.

"Tell me, how miserable did I make her life?" The usual peacefulness that was in her eyes was replaced by a grim look.

"Mark...Brent. Alli is a very lonely girl. She always has been."

"That doesn't answer my question."

"My point is, Brent, that even before you met her, she had a hard life."

"And I just made it that much harder." Brent rubbed his face. There was a long silence that confirmed what he had just stated. "What can you tell me about her home life?" The enchantress just gave a small smile.

"I'm afraid that you'll need to ask Alli that herself. It's not my information to tell." Brent felt as though she was trying to make this conversation harder for him. "So..."

"So what?"

185

"Are you going to give her a chance? By at least trying, you could make her happier than she is now." After another long pause Brent answered her.

"I'll try. But." He spoke quickly when he saw a smile start on the enchantress' face. "But, know that I no longer care. I'll try for her sake. That is all." He stood up suddenly.

"That is all that I ask." Brent narrowed his eyes at her, wondering if there was a deeper meaning to her words somehow. Most likely, there was.

She watched as Brent left the clearing.

"Oh, Mark. You have no idea how much you've changed," she whispered softly.

~*~

After Brent left me outside, I spent the majority of the day alone. I was slightly worried at Brent's reaction. He had looked both defeated and angry at the same time, and it put me on edge. I couldn't understand him. While he had been slowly getting the hang of how to be nicer, his moods were unpredictable. His reaction to hearing about Mark had really stunned me.

I didn't see him at lunch or at dinner, and I was starting to think that he had lied when he told me that he wasn't angry at me.

Over the next several days, I caught only small glimpses of Brent. Sometimes it was him disappearing through a door, or it was during a meal. Finally though, I managed to trap him in the library. Or rather, he had managed to trap me. I was just leaving as he came through the door and I ran straight into him. I let out a gasp as I hit his chest, and another awkward moment followed where I almost fell, but didn't as his arm caught me around the waist and steadied me. My face burned with humiliation as I stepped back away from him. Just how many times would he have to catch me as I fell?

"S-sorry." I twisted my mouth into an unconvincing smile, rubbing my arm where he had touched me. Brent nodded, silent, and made as though to move past me. "Wait!" I threw up my hands in front of me, and I grimaced slightly at the way my voice rose in pitch. "What did I do?"

"What do you mean?" Brent stared at me as though he had never seen me before. Those were the first words I had heard directed at me in several days other than a slight hello. I thought I would go crazy. Joshua and Carter must have been used to Brent's moods, because they didn't seem too concerned at his temporary muteness. All this silence had begun to make me jumpy.

"You're avoiding me and you haven't said a word since we spoke several days ago. Please just tell me what I did wrong! Was it something I did?"

"No." He looked almost surprised. "You didn't do anything." There was an awkward pause.

"Then, what did I say wrong?"

"You didn't do or say anything wrong."

"Then what's the matter?"

"Nothing." I let out a small sigh. He wasn't giving me anything and, judging by the look on his face, he didn't want to be around me at all.

"Okay." My voice came out in small whisper as I quickly brushed past him and disappeared into my room.

I shouldn't have been hurt, but I was. I was in this place because of him, wasn't I? He could at least make an attempt to bear my presence. I felt as though there was a knot inside my chest that was slowly growing tighter.

By the time that night had fallen, I had worked myself up into such a state that I didn't go down to dinner. That night proved to be a very long and hard night. I kept remembering how alone I was here and then there was the matter of my family... It was a continuous cycle that kept me awake. Somewhere in the early hours of the next morning, I realized that I had officially been held captive here for about a month. It seemed like a whole lot longer than that.

Chapter 14

Brent watched Alli's form slip past him and into her room. She looked similar to the way she was when she had first arrived in this cave place: nervous and sad. He knew exactly why she was acting like that, and he knew that it was because of him. Again. Ever since that talk he had with the enchantress, he spent his time trying to figure out how he was supposed to be....normal? That didn't seem like the right word. Nice?

If anything, he was avoiding her because he didn't know how to act. It had been two years since he had tried to just be on a 'friend' basis with a girl. Even then, he wasn't very experienced.

"Man, Brent." Brent turned around to see Joshua leaning against the wall behind him. "Are you trying to get her to leave you alone?"

"No." Brent crossed his arms.

"You sure?" Joshua moved past him into the library, and Brent followed. "Because, from what I can see, she seemed pretty upset at being ignored."

"What do you want me to say? I'm sorry, okay?" There was silence for a moment. "I'm just- I spoke with the enchantress again."

"And?" Joshua's full attention was on Brent now.

"I'll try. Not to break the curse, but to help Allison."

"Call her Alli already. And how exactly do you think you can help her by avoiding her? If you think that she doesn't want to be around you, you're dead wrong. She hates being alone, and Carter and I aren't here most of the time. You've got to be there for her." Brent felt as though he already knew that information, but he stored it away anyway.

When Alli didn't come down to dinner that night, Brent knew it was because of him. He could feel Joshua's eyes boring into his head from across the fire, and he couldn't bring himself to meet his gaze.

The next day, Alli missed both breakfast and lunch, and by the time dinner had rolled around, Brent had already checked to see if she was alright several times in his mirror. Each time, he saw her either painting or just watching the sea. As the dinner bell rang, he noticed a small tear slip down her face, and it suddenly dawned on him that she had been there for a month. She probably missed her family. Knowing that it was all his fault twisted his stomach into knots.

She wasn't showing any sign of getting up to eat something, so he made up his mind. He made a quick detour to the dining room and grabbed his and Alli's plates before heading back up the stairs towards her room. He set the plates down to knock on the closed door and waited. There was nothing.

"Allison? Alli? Can you open the door?" He hated how vulnerable asking made him sound, but he waited a moment longer. He was just opening his mouth once more when the door opened.

There were dark circles under Alli's eye, and for some reason, the sight made Brent pause.

"I'm not hungry." She began to close the door, but Brent stopped it with his foot.

"You need to eat something." Brent got the plates of food off of the ground. "You don't even need to go down. I brought the food up." Alli left the door open behind her as she went back into her room. Brent took this as an invitation to go ahead and enter.

She had been busy. The mural of the mountain used to only cover one wall, but now it covered about half the room. It was wild enough to make him stop in mid-step. There was no way she could have done so much and still made it look so real. He felt as though he could walk through the wall and be transported there. He wished he could. He shook his head to clear it.

"You've done all of this." His words came out as more of a question than the statement he meant it to be.

"Yeah." A moment later, Brent finally remembered to give her the plate. She sat down on the couch, staring at her food. He stood there awkwardly for a moment before she gave him a small smile. "You can sit down if you want." She gestured towards the opposite end of the couch, and Brent sat down. Alli began to eat her food, slowly at first, but then much faster. She was definitely hungry. Brent just picked at his food, mostly looking at the mural. "Thank you." Her soft voice snapped him out of his daze once more. He nodded in acknowledgement, and more silence ensured. "You called me Alli."

"What?" Now Brent was looking at her fully. He thought back to a couple minutes earlier. Oh yeah. He had.

"When you were trying to get me to open the door."

"Oh...I didn't mean..."

"It's fine. I would rather you called me Alli."

"Okay." More silence.

"So...You're not still mad at me?" Brent shook his head.

"I never was."

"We've had this conversation before. But if you weren't angry at me, then why did you avoid me?" Ah. That was the question. How on earth he was going to answer this, Brent had no idea. It's not as though he could blurt out the whole story about how an enchantress made him look like this and that he used to be her worst enemy. He inwardly winced. Yeah. That would not make for a good conversation. He muttered something under his breath.

"What did you say?"

"I was being stupid." Whatever she had been expecting him to say, from the looks on her face, that wasn't it. She gave him a strange look, and he began to open his mouth again, when she spoke.

"Yes, you were." He had not been expecting that, and she must have been able to tell, because she began to giggle slightly. Her laughter made him relax a little. "Just," Her face suddenly turned serious. "Please don't ignore me like that. I hate it." The last part Brent could barely make out, but he understood.

"I won't."

"Brent?" He looked at her. "Can you please tell me why I'm here? I know I made a deal, but why would you guys want me here?" He should have just answered her question from before.

"I-I guess it just gets lonely around here."

"What about Joshua and Carter?"

"Have you ever noticed how they aren't around most of the time?"

"Well, yeah..."

"They have work to do in the city and they are literally never here, except for at mealtimes."

"What kind of work?"

"I believe their work is similar to a charity drive. They help whoever they can."

"Oh." She was quiet for a long time, and Brent wondered if she had taken his words in the wrong way.

"So, you're not seeking female companionship." Brent inwardly winced. He could see how she might take his actions to mean that.

"No. No. No. Nothing like that." He definitely didn't want that. He had thought about it for about five minutes about a year ago, but found that the idea disturbed him too much. He hadn't contemplated it since. "At the most just a friend." He knew that she was probably thinking that his way of basically blackmailing her into spending the summer here in order to be friends with him was completely psychotic. It was better than telling her that she was supposed to fall in love with him.

"Why didn't you just say that before?" Because it sounded crazy? He told her as much, but she just shook her head. "You don't get it. I've been waiting for something bad to happen for a month. If you had told me this before, I might not have been so scared of you."

"You're not scared of me anymore?" He wondered if she meant to use past tense.

"No." She spoke slowly. "You are intimidating, but no, I'm not scared of you anymore."

"What changed?" She gave a small shrug. "You did."

~*~

I knew that as soon as I told Brent that he had changed, he didn't know how to respond. I had caught him off guard. I had caught him off guard before, but this time, he seemed to be more affected. It was like there was some type of war inside him. I wondered why.

Part of me was a little freaked out that he was going to just get up and leave, like he had all of the other times, but he didn't.

A silence fell over us once more, but this time it wasn't awkward. The silence belonged in the moment. I took the time to study the wall. Brent had

194

been so startled and amazed at how much had been done since the last time he had been in here, the effect was almost comical. It truly was magical. I knew for sure that there was magic working as I painted. Sure, I did the work of moving the brush, but I had noticed the way the paint dried darker in certain spots to create a 3-D effect, and it wasn't because of me. This place was definitely magical, and the magic was charming.

~*~

The next morning, I woke to find that there was barely any sunlight at all coming through the window. A major storm was about to be unleashed over the sea. When I looked to my mural, I found, much to my surprise, that there wasn't a single sight of rain in them. I guess that after seeing it reflect the time of day outside so many times, I also expected it to show the weather. It was a strange contrast. In my room it looked like the perfect day, while outside, it looked as though the heavens were going to cry.

After several moments, I shook my head at the strange sight and left my room to brave the hall. It wasn't a surprise to me when I ran into Brent again. He had been exiting the library right as I walked by. This time, I managed to jump back before we slammed together.

"Morning." I spoke first. Brent blinked once before returning my reply with:

"Do you still need that on your ankle?" I glanced down and saw that he was talking about the ankle brace I had been wearing.

195

"Nice conversation starter." I said dryly. In all honesty, I had forgotten that I had been wearing that thing. Brent grimaced a little, and I let out a small chuckle. He was too easy to tease. "But, to answer your question, I have no idea." I turned my body towards the medical room. "Do we need to..."

"Not immediately. After breakfast?"

"Sure." We really needed better conversations. Brent gestured for me to lead the way to the dining area, and we continued on in silence. I began to open my mouth to say something, when the bell rang. Thank goodness. I got off of the steps and froze in place. For the first time, it wasn't me running into Brent, but him running into me.

He still had to make sure that I didn't fall over, but my eyes were locked firmly on the sight in front of me.

"Brent!" I grabbed his arm without looking. "Are you seeing this?" Judging by his sudden intake of breath, he was.

There was a person standing in front of the fire. It wasn't even a person at that. It was more like looking at a bright orange glow in the shape of something human. And it was holding one of the plates of food. The flame person saw us and held out the plate toward us.

"Brent?" I hated the nervousness in my voice, and immediately cleared my throat, but it didn't help much.

"It's back." I wasn't expecting that.

"What's ba- Oh." Joshua came to a halt as he walked in. I swore that I saw a partial smile on his face, but it disappeared when he looked at Brent. Brent did not look like a happy camper. I got the impression that he wanted to throttle the fire figure. That couldn't be a good thing for either of them.

I looked back to the fire and let out a yelp, almost propelling myself into Brent. I hadn't even seen the thing move, but there it was, about two feet away, still holding the plate of food.

"Brent!" I yelped. "What is that thing?"

"Not exactly sure." He spoke dryly, as though he was unsure about how he felt being the barrier between me and the fire-thing. I wondered if he was rolling his eyes. He took the plate it offered and with a small puff of extra fire, the thing disappeared.

"Does it have a name?" Brent gave me a look that told me all I needed to know. I glanced back to the fire. The figure was back again, waving another plate in Joshua's face. Joshua looked strangely happy at the sight of the strange creature and took the plate. The next time the figure appeared, I got to take the plate. To my surprise, the figure gave a huge smile and bowed before disappearing.

"Why have I never seen Flame Head before?"

"Flame Head?" Carter walked into the room, but quickly pulled to a stop the Flame Head popped into existence right in front of him. He let out a groan before taking the plate of food.

"Why is it back?"

"What is wrong with Flame Head?"

"Nothing." Joshua seemed pleased.

"Brent?" I turned questioningly towards him, hoping for more explanation. By this time, he had made his way to his seat and was sitting down slowly as though waiting for something to happen.

"Nothing's wrong...yet." Perfect. What was that supposed to mean?

To my greatest annoyance, I couldn't get anything else out of anyone for the rest of the meal, or the rest of the day, for that matter. I was learning that men were not good at answering questions. After lunch, I took the brace off of my now-healed ankle, but by this time I wasn't surprised. Of course magic was involved.

~*~

Breakfast and lunch the next day were also served by Flame Head, whose name I had shortened down to just Flame. It was really quite amusing to see the glares that Brent and Carter kept sending the over-excited creature, but they still wouldn't tell me why they despised it so much. I still spent the majority of my time in the library, but the job of organizing was quickly becoming tedious.

At times when I could no longer stand it, I would pick up a book and begin reading. I had found an old copy of Grimm's Fairy Tales, and it was now my official go-to book. I loved the stories.

About an hour after lunch had ended, I looked up from my book briefly and sucked in a short breath of surprise when I saw Brent casually browsing the shelf next to me. It was one of the few shelves that had any organization whatsoever.

198

"When did you get in here?" There was no way I couldn't have heard him enter, and yet, here he was. Brent gave me a glance over his shoulder, before turning back to the shelf and choosing a book.

"About an hour ago."

"What?" I had left the dining area before he had.

"Need I repeat myself?" Somehow Brent's tone hadn't changed once as he looked at the book in his hands. He sounded almost bored.

"No, I mean, how--you know what. Never mind." It wasn't worth it. I shook my head as Brent put the book back and pulled another book off the shelf. I paused to observe his actions. "Are you even looking at the titles on those books?"

"No." I let out a brief laugh before catching myself. Brent moved the books on the shelves around at random, as though too bored to do anything. I suddenly understood how the library got to be so chaotic in the first place.

"Hey. Stop that!" I sat up immediately, startling Brent, causing him to fumble with the book he was pulling out and drop it.

"What?" He turned to me with a frown on his face, but I was too ticked to care.

"What do you think you're doing? I've spent all this time, trying to organize these shelves, and you come in here and mix them all up again!?" Brent looked completely confused, well, as confused as he had ever looked in front of me, but I was too irritated to care.

"Um-I wasn't mixing them up." I narrowed my eyes.

"Then what do you call taking books off the shelf at random and putting them back in a different place." As I spoke, the annoyance in my voice began to switch to a horribly suppressed giggle. I tried to cover my mouth some, but it didn't help at all. I wasn't sure, but I'm sure that he just grew more confused. I took a deep breath to recover and stood up. "I have the perfect punishment. From now on, you get to help me fix the mess you make." Brent's eyes narrowed a little.

"I do, now, do I?"

"Yes. You do." I could see hesitation in his eyes briefly, before he conceded with a small nod of the head.

~*~

"Brent! Keep those books on the shelf!" I was exhausted from how hard it was to get Brent to pay attention to what he was doing. I had no idea he had such a distracted mindset. He hadn't stopped shifting stuff around since I had put him to work, and only about half of what he did helped. The other half made the mess worse. How had I not noticed this before? "You need to-" My words were cut off by the sound of the dinner bell ringing loudly. "Finally!" I exclaimed, standing up. I was already halfway out the door by the time Brent had gotten off of the floor, exasperated.

I heard him mumbling something behind me, but refused to be goaded. I did my best to keep my eyes focused straight ahead with a straight face, but it was proving to be very difficult.

As was now becoming a routine, Flame brought each person their plate, but when I held out my hands to take the food, I found that in place of my food was a small round cake with *Happy Birthday* written on the top in icing. Confusion filled my mind as I tried to figure out the day, and then it dawned on me.

"Wait! It's July fourth, isn't it!"

"You have a fourth of July birthday?" I looked at Brent with surprise.

"Yes, but how did I end up with a cake?"

"Magic." Joshua spoke up from across the fire.

"Well, that was a no-brainer." I mumbled, deadpanning.

"17?" I nodded in reply to Carter's question.

"Yep. Sweet sixteen is done and gone." I gave a small smile at the cake and my stomach growled. I looked up. "Is there a way to get something besides just cake for dinner?" I saw amusement in Brent's eyes, but it soon disappeared when Flame popped up right in front of me, holding another plate out to me, full of brownies. "Ummm." I looked unsurely at the plate. "Something else?"

Flame wouldn't go away until I took the plate, and when he did, he was holding another plate with pie on it. Joshua began to chuckle at the look on my face. I think I understood why Brent and Carter had both scowled at Flame when he had appeared.

"Thanks." I took the plate and set it on the floor with the other desserts, and Flame disappeared. I looked up at the three guys around me. Brent's eyes were lit up with contained laughter at my predicament. "Dessert anyone?"

~*~

Flame Head, or Flame as Alli called it, was driving Brent crazy already. Each time he came into the dining area, whether it was a meal time or not, the fiery creature would pop up and try to shove a plate of food into his hands.

Brent had thought that when Flame had disappeared a year ago that the thing would be gone for good, but it was obviously not meant to be. He might have been able to bear Flame's presence if not for Joshua. Joshua loved Flame, merely because he drove Carter and Brent crazy.

He kind of wondered how long Alli would last with no one telling her why they hated (or, in Joshua's case, loved) Flame so much, but he wasn't willing to explain what exactly had led up to several days of no food and many empty plates.

Alli spent most of her time in the library, organizing. He never really understood why she had chosen that task. Of all of the things she could have done instead, she decided to move books around. She would never survive.

He actually felt kind of bad watching her fix up the shelves. He was, after all, the entire reason that the books were everywhere in the first place. But, when he tried to help out, he was always painfully aware of Alli's gaze boring into the back of his head. He could barely focus on what he was doing as he moved books around. Apparently it was much harder to be on 'friendly' terms with her than he originally thought. He had no clue where to begin.

Brent shook his head slightly to clear his thoughts and tried to focus on his food, but he was having a hard time concentrating. Alli truly looked bewildered at the three desserts around her. The first time that had happened to him, there were quite a few more than just three dessert plates. He had to admit: she was handling this much better than any of them had.

"I wish I could have some more food." Brent jerked slightly out of his daze when Joshua spoke loudly, holding his half-finished plate behind his back while staring at the fire. What was he thinking?

A moment later, he found out. Flame burst into existence with a wide smile and another plate of food, which Joshua took with his free hand. As soon as Flame was gone, he passed the full plate to Alli, who took it gratefully.

"And that, Gentlemen, is why I am on good terms with Flame Head."

"Sure." Carter glared at him, Brent rolled his eyes, and Alli started laughing. Nothing new there. But, it was her birthday. Brent thought for a moment. There just might be something he could do for her.

~*~

"Hey, Alli." I smiled to myself when I noticed that Brent had called me by my nickname and came to a stop outside my door.

"Yeah?"

"Let me show you something." Brent waited for a moment to make sure that I was following him before leading the way to the portal outside.

The night air was much warmer than inside with almost no breeze. The stars could be clearly seen, but it wasn't the stars that drew my attention. There was a sudden flash of color in the distance near the town.

I quickly ran over to the cliffside and watched the sky light up with fireworks. It was almost as though I had my own show, done just for me. I had never seen fireworks from such a distance. It was beautiful.

"Happy birthday." Brent's voice came softly from behind me. I tore my eyes away from the sight and smiled at him.

"Thank you."

Chapter 15

As much as I would have loved to just watch the colorful fireworks every night after that, the next couple of days dawned misty and grey. I found myself back to undertaking the idle work in the library once more. Brent would come and join me sometimes, reading in one of the various armchairs. Whenever he saw that I was getting ticked off, he would pitch in by sticking books onto half-empty shelves.

The trouble with his help, is that he did everything at random. Part of me was glad that he cared enough to help, but the majority of me wanted to throw one of the books at him. There was no organization in him at all.

By the third day after my birthday, I was done being patient.

"Brent! Please stop!" I let out a groan and pulled myself off of the ground where I was sitting. "Your help doesn't help."

Brent didn't reply, only looked at me once before his hand shoved another book on the shelf. I narrowed my eyes.

"Ugghhh! I wish these book would just shelve themselves!" I threw the book in my hand to the ground. It was useless. I was done. "Gahh!" I threw a hand up in front of my face and jerked back, landing on my rear as the book came flying past my face. I watched as the book settled on the top shelf of one of the bookcases. "What the heck? Brent?"

"What did you just do?" Brent seemed just as startled as I was.

"That's not normal?"

"No. That's not normal at all."

"Good, I thought I was going crazy." He mumbled something that I didn't catch, but I decided to let it slip.

"Try it again."

"Wait. You want me to throw a book again?"

"Yes." Correction. He was crazy. I picked up another random book and tossed it at the ground. It landed with a loud thump. "No! Throw it like you did last time, with force." I glared at him. He probably wanted me to look like an idiot.

I grabbed another book and dropped it straight down. An annoyed look crossed Brent's face. Good. That made two of us angry.

"You're doing it wrong." I'd show him wrong. I grabbed another book.

"You do it then." I tossed the book at him like a frisbee and, inches from his chest, it veered away and flew to a different nearby shelf. "Huh." I stared at the now shelved book. "This should be fun."

"Tons." Judging from his tone, he probably thought I was going to keep throwing books at him until they all went on the bookshelf. Well, he wouldn't be far off from the truth. I picked up another book.

~*~

I stopped in my tracks as I arrived in the dining area. "There's a window."

"Thanks, Captain Obvious." Carter grinned as I glared at him, and I turned my gaze back to the giant window in the wall of the dining area.

There was now a window that rose from my waist to about the top of Brent's head and the length of the entire wall on the west side of the dining room. It was divided up into three sections by small stone columns, but that detail didn't register as quickly as the view the window revealed.

"How the heck are we able to see the forest from here?"

"Magic!" I turned to face Joshua.

"No way. I thought that there was a giant TV screen that was fooling me this whole time." Joshua didn't say anything in reply, but I saw Carter smirking at my words. Good to know that he approved.

"There's a window." Brent's voice came from the stairs as I stuck my head out of the window. I pulled it back in and replied dryly, "Thanks, Captain Obvious." I leaned back out to get a better look as Carter cracked up laughing.

I wondered if I would be able to get outside through the window, but my efforts proved fruitless when I found that I couldn't get my lower body past the ledge. At the most I could sit on the window sill.

"There has got to be something in that library that could explain this."

"Good luck finding it." Brent must have been still irritated that I was using him as target practice with books yesterday.

"Oh, don't feel bad about being singled out. I will need plenty of help, and since those two," I pointed at Joshua and Carter, who both looked amused, "aren't available, you are the default."

"You're referring to me as a default?" I wanted to laugh at the slightly offended tone in Brent's voice.

"Yep."

"Brilliant."

I eventually wandered back to the library just before Brent. I pick up a book and looked at it for a moment before throwing it like a frisbee. It smacked into a shelf and fell to the ground. I glared at the offending object. Right. It looked like I would be using Brent for target practice after all. Whenever I threw books at him, they almost never hit him.

I don't think Brent completely trusted me to do this, since the last time, a rather large book had slammed into his shoulder.

I heard the door to the library open and smiled.

"Hey, Brent! I could use a little help with these books!" This would be fun.

~*~

Later, I was once again reading some of Grimm's Fairy Tales, although this version was different from the one I usually read and had several new stories. One crazy story that I found was called *A Tall Tale From Ditmarsh*, but I had to stop. It made no sense whatsoever, and I was giggling too hard.

"What are you laughing at?" I had to calm myself down before I could speak clearly to Brent. In the end, I just pointed to the story and had him read it himself.

A Tall Tale From Ditmarsh

I want to tell you something. I saw two roasted chickens flying swiftly with their breasts turned toward heaven, their backs toward hell. An anvil and millstone swam across the Rhine very slowly and softly, and a frog sat on the ice eating a plowshare at Pentecost. There were three fellows on crutches and stilts who wanted to catch a hare. One was deaf, the second blind, the third dumb, and the fourth could not move either foot. Do you want to know how they did it? Well, first the blind one saw the hare trotting over the field. Then the dumb one called to the lame one, and the lame one caught the hare by the collar. There were some men who wanted to sail on land. They set their sails in the wind and sailed across the wide fields. As they sailed over a high mountain they were miserably drowned. A crab chased a hare, making it flee, and high on a roof was a cow who had climbed on top of it. In that country the flies are as large as the goats here. Open the window so the lies can fly out.[2]

"What?" He looked up after reading it with such a look of confusion on his face that I began to giggle again.

"I don't know."

"What are you reading?"

"*The Complete Fairy Tales of the Brothers Grimm.*"

"That's a fairy tale?" Brent didn't look too convinced. I laughed again and took the book from him.

"Not all of the fairy tales are about princesses." I flipped to a different story. "Here, read this one."

"*All Fur?*" I nodded.

"Read it aloud." I settled back in the chair to get myself more comfortable. Brent raised an eyebrow, but read anyway.

By the time dinner came about, we had gone through about three more stories, and I could tell

Brent wasn't sure if he was enjoying himself or not. For some reason, the temperature had dropped in the library, and I was thankful for the excuse to go to sit next to the bonfire at dinner.

After another meal served by Flame, Joshua and Carter left for the night while Brent and I headed back to the library. When I entered, I stopped short.

"Since when was there a fireplace here?" Brent didn't answer. He didn't need to.

I walked over to the fireplace. I knew that the chairs had been facing the bookshelves, but now the chairs were positioned around the fireplace. The area near the fire was completely clean of random stacks of books, and the only book next to the armchairs was the book of fairy tales.

I plopped down into one of the armchairs and look up at Brent.

"I like this." I smile, and after a hesitation, he smiled back at me. The sight was enough to make me happy for the rest of the night. I ended up falling asleep right in the middle of one of the stories that Brent was reading with a warm feeling in my chest.

~*~

"Come on! It's your turn to read and you know it!" I pleaded with Carter, but he just crossed his arms.

"I'm tired."

I huffed at Carter.

"Of course you're tired! That's what the human body does when it's been awake for several hours. Come on! Another hour won't kill you, you

211

baby!" I had learned over the past month that in order to get Carter to respond to me, I had to use sarcasm and dry humor. I was starting to wonder if he enjoyed the banter and was dragging it out longer than needed.

"Get up, you lazy butt." Joshua smacked the back of Carter's head as he walked by, finally getting him to stand up and follow the rest of us up to the library.

"You first!" I cheerfully handed Carter the Grimm's Fairy Tales book, and he looked at it with a disgusted look.

"Fairy tales? You've got to be kidding me."

"Just read it already!" He was starting to drive me crazy.

Finally, Carter began a fairytale at random, and, to the amusement of everyone, he seemed to get himself pretty drawn into the story. He ended up reading five before I relieved him of the book and gave it to Brent. I hid a smile at the look of surprise on Carter's face when he realized how long he had been reading.

In the next few days, I was sure his perspective would change regarding fairy tales. Some were a whole lot darker than most people thought, but all were entertaining to say the least. There was a reason why I loved them.

~*~

A couple nights later, I took pity on Joshua and Carter and let them have an early night, although Carter put up more protest than I thought he might. Eventually, it was just Brent and I sitting

212

by the fire on the floor. It was a quiet night, and neither of us felt like reading aloud for the moment.

I was on my stomach, resting on my elbows, when I turned to Brent.

"What's your favorite color?" Brent gave me a look. "What? It's a perfectly reasonable conversation starter." I defended my question. Brent rolled his eyes. "How about this. You answer my questions, and I'll answer yours."

"What makes you think I've got questions about you?"

"Of course you do." I rolled my eyes. "Now answer the question."

"Green. What's your favorite color?"

"Are you kidding me?" The hypocrite. "Blue. Ever had any pets?"

"Nope, unless you count the imaginary bird I played with when I was six." I snorted in laughter. "Any pets on your end?" I had to think for a moment.

"My brother used to bring home strays all of the time. I believe we once had a total of two dogs, three cats, and a turtle all at one time. The only pet I personally owned was a hermit crab, which died when my brother accidentally boiled it in its shell while giving it a bath." Brent looked a little startled at that information, and I let out a chuckle.

"How old are you?" I had actually been wondering about this for a while, but never had the chance to ask. Brent started to say something, but seemed to change his mind.

"21." I wondered what he was about to say before, but he asked his next question too quickly. "What's your best childhood memory?" I went through my memories. The older I got, the harder it was to remember the good ones.

"I think," I began slowly. "the best memory I have is one from when I was really young. It was Christmas, and the whole family, even my dad, had fallen asleep, piled on the couch after watching *It's a Wonderful Life*. I remember waking up, and everyone just seemed so joyful. I can't remember a happier time." I shook myself out of memory lane. "So, what was your favorite book as a kid?"

"Of course you would ask that." He thought for a moment. "I was never a huge reader, but when I did read, I read books that had adventures, like Batman and Superman." I glanced at him with a funny look on my face.

"Aren't those just comic books?" He shrugged. I thought about my next question and smiled. "What was the most embarrassing thing that ever happened to you when you went to school?" Brent winced as though he knew exactly what it was.

"I was pranked in the lunchroom. Someone covered my seat with honey and I sat in it. It led to quite a few nicknames for a couple of months." I covered my mouth to stop from laughing. He scowled at me.

"I knew a boy who had a similar thing happen to him. Only, he also ended up with a bunch of whip cream on his head, and I got blamed. It was totally worth it."

"Wait, you pulled that prank?" I nodded.

"I was only in charge of the whip cream. The honey...I'm still not sure who ended up putting it on the chair." Brent shook his head.

"Who was your first crush?" I let my head drop for a moment while I groaned.

"I hate this question. It's too complicated." Brent just smiled. "It was a movie actor in middle school, and, no, I won't tell you who, but then once I was in high school, there was a boy who looked similar to the actor, but then he treated me like crap, so I stayed away from him."

"What did he do?" Brent was frowning slightly, and I smiled at him, trying to ignore an odd flutter in my chest.

"He waited until we were in public before humiliating me." I gave a wry grin. "I learned my lesson after that to be careful who I fell for. I haven't fallen for anyone since."

"I'm sorry." I shrugged.

"It's not your fault that some people are jerks." Brent was still frowning, and I found my stomach doing a flip flop when I realized that he was angry for me.

We fell silent after that, and, after about ten minutes of silence, I stood up.

"Night, Brent." I gave him a sleepy smile.

"Goodnight, Alli." A small thrill ran through my body when he smiled at me.

~*~

215

"Brent, I can't stand being stuck inside for a moment longer!" I groaned loudly and threw the book in my hands at him. It flew to a bookshelf, even though I had been secretly hoping it would just hit him already. I couldn't get the books to hit him anymore, and I only felt a little sorry for aiming at his head. An idea came to mind. "I can go back outside alone now, right?"

That got Brent's attention more so than the flying book had. He had taken to looking up at me whenever I threw a book at him with an amused look on his face that was almost smug.

"It might still be dangerous." Brent warned.

I shrugged. "Then come with me." Brent looked he wasn't sure he wanted to come outside. "Come on!" I stood up and grabbed his arm, tugging him up.

"But..." Brent's protest was useless, and he quickly gave in and allowed me to pull him out of the library, his book still in his hand. The hypocrite obviously didn't care if he was outside or not.

~*~

Brent really didn't care if he was reading inside or outside. Hence the smile on his face that Alli couldn't see as she pulled him to the library entrance.

Before, he had always come outside to get away from the darkness of the cave and give himself the illusion of freedom. It was rare that he came outside for pleasure, but he had to admit to himself that it was a nice change of scenery. Alli let go of his hand once they reached the clearing, and he walked

216

away from her a small bit and sat down at the base of one of the larger trees and reopened his book. His clinched his hand that she had been holding, still able to feel the leftover warmth of her touch.

For a moment, everything was peaceful, but at the sound of a large crack, he looked up.

"I'm all right!" Alli shouted over her shoulder as she slowly tried to loop a leg over the branch above her head. She was going to kill herself trying to climb that tree.

"What are you doing?" Brent leaned forwards, wondering if she was going to fall. She was definitely accident prone, and that particular fall could only end badly.

"Almost got it." Alli huffed as she got both legs over the branch. She let her arms take a break as she swung by her knees. Brent stood up. He knew from experience that she was going to need help.

"Are you sure about that?" Brent gave a smirk as Alli glared at him from her position.

"Yes," she said curtly, before straining to get onto the branch. A moment later, she was back to swinging. "You know what?" She spoke breathlessly. "I don't think I like climbing this tree anymore." Brent gave a small chuckle.

"Here." He gave her the push she needed to get on the branch. "Next time, try climbing a different tree." Alli smiled from her perch.

"Nah." She brushed his logical idea away. "I'll just have to make sure you're here to help whenever I climb instead." He rolled his eyes and left her to climb the rest of the tree on her own.

217

"You know, you should get outside more." I spoke to Brent, who was once more sitting under his tree, reading. I had never realized that he spent so much time with books. That was usually my forte.

He looked up from where he was sitting.

"I am outside." I inwardly groaned. He knew that wasn't what I meant.

"No..." I trailed off and frowned.

"No...What?" I held a finger up to my lips and cocked my head in the direction I thought I had heard the noise. He must have heard it as well, for a few seconds later, he jumped to his feet. "Get down!" He spoke in a harsh whisper, and I hurried to do so.

Brent was helping me down from the last branch when it became clear that the voices weren't those of the killers. I could hear high laughter, like that of a child. There were adult voices coming from farther away calling for the kid.

Brent pulled me quickly towards the portal and we were soon through, but not before I heard a small voice asking who we were.

Once inside, I sucked in a deep breath to calm myself down. I hadn't realized how much adrenaline was coursing through my body.

"Why did we run?"

"Alli. People aren't scared of you, but did it not cross your mind that if that little girl had seen me, she would have screamed?" There was a dark undertone to his words. I had forgotten about his scars. I guess he did have a point there.

"I'm sorry," I spoke in a soft voice and placed a hand on his arm. "I didn't think. I forgot about your scars." I don't think Brent was expecting that reply because he fell silent.

~*~

I couldn't get the echo of the young girl's laughter out of my head. Each time I heard it in my head, memories of childhood would come to mind. They were happy memories, but I couldn't dwell on them for long without getting a hollow feeling in my chest. It took a while, but I finally figured out that I was homesick. Of course, now that I knew that, I couldn't get the idea of home out of my head.

I think that Brent had started to get a little worried about me. Ever since we almost got caught outside, I had become a bit quieter. I hadn't asked to go back outside either, so he knew something was up. He gave me some space for several days and was, for the most part, silent around me.

"Alli." I looked up from the book in my lap to see Brent sitting across from me in front if the fireplace.

"Yeah?" Part of me wondered how long he had been sitting there. There wasn't a book in his hands. Brent let out a small breath.

"What's going on?" So, he was finally going to get on my case for being quiet.

"Nothing." I suddenly felt bad. Here I was moping about wanting to leave when he couldn't even leave this place if he wanted to. I wondered if he had family that he wanted to see as well. "I'm fine."

"You want to leave, don't you?" To say that I was stunned would be an understatement. It looks like he's better at connecting pieces than I had thought. I was silent for a little bit, before I wet my lips in order to speak.

"I only want to see my family." Brent nodded as though he understood. My voice dropped even quieter and I looked down at the closed book on my lap. "Can I please visit them?" There was more silence.

"Not in person." Brent's voice was rougher than usual. "If you wish to send a letter, you can give it to either Joshua or Carter to deliver, but besides that, you may know that they are safe and are doing well. There isn't any sign of your father."

"Okay." I bit my lip, feeling foolish for having asked. When I looked up from my lap, Brent was already disappearing out of the door. My chest suddenly grew tight as I thought at how upset he had sounded.

After that conversation, neither Brent nor I really spoke much to each other over the following days. The silence was making me nervous. I felt as though it was the calm before the storm, only I didn't know what form the storm was going to take. Joshua and Carter could tell that something was going on between us, and, as a result, fireside conversations were strained and quieter. On the days that they were missing, there were no conversations at all.

I spent the two month mark alone in my room. Again. Maybe history really is destined to repeat itself.

Chapter 16

"What did you do?" Brent let out a long sigh before facing Joshua. Dinner was just being served, and Alli's place was once more empty.

"Why is that whenever something happens, you assume it's because of me?" Joshua shrugged.

"Well, did you do something?" Brent scowled and stared into the fire.

"No."

"Are you sure?"

"Of course not!"

"Nice answer." Joshua smirked before his face went serious again. "So, what happened? She gave me a letter two days ago to drop off, but hasn't said a word to me since."

"She's getting homesick."

"I see."

"No, you don't, Joshua!" Brent buried his face in his hands. "We only have about a month left! Why is she even here? There is no hope!" Joshua stared hard at Brent.

"Brent, you can't truthfully tell me that you don't feel something towards her."

"And what makes you think that?"

"Just because she can't see you smiling at her when her back is turned doesn't mean Carter and I can't." Brent opened his mouth to protest, but couldn't. Joshua was telling the truth. "Listen, Brent. You are falling for her, even though you may not know it. You may have lost hope, but Carter and I are still holding out." Sometimes it was hard to forget that Joshua and Carter were under the same curse as him. "But even if you don't think about the curse, think about Alli. She's also here because of the curse." Brent felt as though there was plenty more that could be said, but he couldn't think of a single thing to say. "You might also want to bring her food. She probably hasn't eaten at all today."

"Right." Brent got up from his seat and went to take Alli's plate up to her. He paused at the doorway. "You're trying to set us up, aren't you?"

"Of course I am." Joshua shot him an evil smile. "I thought you would know that by now." Brent realized that it was kind of a stupid question to ask and escaped the room feeling foolish. Joshua had a way with words that fooled people into thinking that he understood a whole lot more than what he really knew.

When Brent reached Alli's room, he used his foot to knock, and not five seconds later, Alli opened the door. By the look on her face, she must have been expecting him.

"You brought food." Brent raised an eyebrow.

"Is it that obvious?" She ducked her head slightly and laughed quietly. Brent felt slightly pleased with himself for making her laugh.

"Come on in." Alli opened the door wider, and the two were soon seated on the couch. When Brent sat down, he shot a confused look her way.

"I don't remember the couch being so..."

"...Soft? Bouncy? Hammocky?" Alli tried to fill in the correct word for him.

"Hammocky?" Brent was almost certain that wasn't a word. "I guess that word would work." Alli shrugged and sat down next to him.

"I think it has to do with the magic." There was silence.

"Look." Brent took a deep breath. "I'm sorry about avoiding you."

~*~

I had to admit: I was not expecting Brent to come outright and apologize. I had been anticipating at least five minutes of awkwardness before either of us would begin to act casual once more.

"It's alright." I bit my lip. "I'm sorry that I made you upset." I really didn't want to upset Brent, I just hadn't been expecting him to act that way towards my question. From what I had gathered, if I tried to leave, they wouldn't force me back, but my mom would stop getting better. So I had to stay here, but what did they gain from that if they didn't want to use me? I remembered that Brent had told me that my being here had to do with the magic I saw, and I knew that Brent couldn't leave this place,

225

and there were boundaries he couldn't cross outside, that is excluding that one time with the killers in the woods. He must be cursed.

Suddenly, everything began to come together.

"Alli?" I was pulled out of my thoughts to find Brent looking at me with concern in his eyes. I stared back with wide eyes, the food on my plate completely forgotten.

"You're cursed, aren't you?" I could have sworn time froze just then by the way Brent stiffened and pulled back slightly. "You can't leave this place at all, but you want to. How did I not see this before? That's why I'm here, isn't it? You want me to try to break your curse!" I stood up quickly, thoughts bouncing around in my head, while Brent just stayed silent and watched me. "But how on earth would I know how to do that? Is that why you are so interested in the library? Do you think that it holds the answers to this magic?" When I fell silent at this question, silence reigned.

"Yes."

It was all Brent said, but the simplicity of his answer astonished me. The way he said it was so haunted and broken, I almost didn't believe that it came from him. It was as though now that I knew why I was here, he expected me to get up and leave.

"Well, how much of the library have you covered?" Brent stared at me as though I had grown a second head. I realized that he really did expect me to get up and leave. I sat back down on the couch. "You know I'm going to help you, right?"

226

"Why?" He spoke so quietly, I could barely hear him.

"I would do no less for someone I consider a friend." I only just now realized the truth of my words.

"You would consider me a friend?" Brent phrased the question as a statement of disbelief. "You don't consider me the blackmailing psycho anymore?" He brought up a good point.

"Yeah, I'm still not a fan of being blackmailed, but you've never done anything to hurt me and you've done everything in your power to protect me. Heck, you took a bullet for me. That's more than what most friends would ever do for each other without a second thought." I paused. "At least, that's what my experience has been."

"Then whoever you're talking about wasn't a true friend." I gave a small smile to him.

"In that case, you just told me that a true friend does exactly what you have done for me." I was kind of proud of myself for coming up with that logical twist to turn the tables on him. I think he could tell, because he shook his head and gave me a small smile.

~*~

It was as if that moment was a turning point for Brent. He seemed more at peace and relaxed than before. Several times over the next couple of days, I caught him smiling. Once, I even managed to make him laugh, which thrilled me to no end and gave me a warm feeling that lasted the whole day.

227

Both of us spent almost all of the time that we had together in the library, combing shelves for an answer to the curse. We gathered all of the books we could find that were related to anything mystical and magical, which wasn't much. The majority of the books in the library consisted of classics and literature that dealt more with humanity's questions than fairytales.

I thought that everything was going pretty well, considering how long we had actually begun the search in earnest, but it became clear that I was missing part of the picture a couple days later.

I was walking down to the dining area from my room to have dinner when I heard raised voices.

"....useless! Why bother complaining? You don't do anything to help!" Brent's voice was clearly furious, and I raced down the last of the stairs just as Carter overturned one of the chairs in frustration.

"You know there isn't a choice on our part!"

I scooted around the pair to where Joshua was standing, casually observing the pair.

"What's going on?" I spoke to him as I watched the other two shout at each other. It's a good thing I knew Brent. Otherwise, I would be terrified of him right now.

"Temper tantrums." I turned to look at Joshua, but he didn't look like he was kidding. "You should put an end to it before they start using their fists instead of their words."

"Me?!" He had to be joking.

228

"Yes, you." Joshua sounded like he was stating the obvious. "Do you really think they would listen to me? And, you might want to hurry." I looked up in time to see Carter sock Brent right in the jaw.

"Stop!" I had seen several fights start this way and they didn't ever end up well, for either party involved. I ran towards them as Brent prepared to lunge and return Carter's gift in full. I grabbed onto Brent as best I could, trying to hold him back. Of course, if he really wanted to, he could easily throw me to the ground like a rag doll, but I knew he wouldn't go that far.

"Alli..." Brent was still tense as a spring as he tried to peel me away from him, but I hung on to him like he was my lifeline.

"Please stop! Please don't hit him!" For a moment, I thought that he was going to relax, but then I heard Carter mumble something. Brent immediately took several steps forward, literally carrying me along. I shut my eyes tightly. "Please!" Without my permission, my voice cracked dangerously as I spoke.

Brent's motion came to an immediate halt, and I could feel his hands on my shoulders. This time, I did nothing to resist him as he pulled me away from his body. I pleaded with him through my eyes, and he must have caught something of my desperation.

"Okay." He spoke softly. "I won't hit him. Even if he does deserve it." The last part was said in a grudging way, but I just shook my head and threw myself back around him, squeezing him tightly.

"Thank you." After a couple of beats, Brent wrapped his arms around me in return. When I pulled away, I avoided looking anyone in the eyes as I went to sit down with my food.

That dinner was a very quiet one, but I still saw the silent looks that the three guys passed between themselves. They seemed to be holding a conversation that I couldn't hear personally. As a result, I left early so they could talk aloud when it became clear they weren't going to do that in my presence.

~*~

As soon as Alli was out of their hearing range, Carter began to hum the wedding march.

"Shut up," Brent all but snarled at him, not that it affected Carter in any way.

"You know," Carter stopped in the middle of his tune. "For the longest time, I thought that there was no hope for you, but now..."

"Shut up." Brent glared at Carter.

"He is right you know." Joshua spoke up. "You've changed. Two months ago, or even one month ago, you never would have hugged her." Brent wanted to say something against that statement, but knew Joshua was right. That didn't mean that he would let them know that though. He stood up.

"Honestly though, Mark?" The use of his first name made Brent freeze, and he turned back to face Carter. "Is it enough? I can't stay here forever."

Joshua's head snapped up at Carter's words. The way Carter looked at Brent made his throat tighten. Brent wasn't the only one affected by the curse. Both Joshua and Carter were cursed just as much as he was.

"I don't know." His words were strained as they came out.

~*~

"Stupid."

I peeked around the corner of the bookshelf once more and stared at Brent. He had been muttering small words of frustration under his breath whenever he thought I couldn't hear, but I had better hearing than he had counted on.

He was currently pinching the bridge of his nose, eyes squeezed shut in aching discomfort. If he thought that I was going to let him continue to hide like that, well, he was mistaken.

I quickly rounded the corner and plopped down on the floor facing him. He opened his eyes too late to hide reality. There was a glassy look to them.

"What hurts?"

"Nothing." His voice was rougher than usual. Brent stood up quickly and immediately grabbed a bookshelf to keep from falling over. I got to my feet to help steady him.

"Liar." I reached up a hand to feel his forehead. He pulled back. "Hold still." I tried again, and, much to my dismay, I was right about him having a fever. "Alright. Let's get you to the medical room."

231

"I'm fine." I rolled my eyes.

"Liar." Brent offered no more protest as I led him to find some medicine.

His fever lasted for about a week, and that time was almost torture. If I weren't so annoyed with Brent for trying to evade the medical room, I would have found it very amusing. The problem was the medicine. In order to keep his temperature down, there was some kind of ointment that I was supposed to rub on his forehead three times a day. It would act like a cool cloth, but Brent seemed to really hate it. He was supposed to stay in the medical room, but I often found him in the library or trying to get outside.

Of course, Joshua and Carter both found it hilarious, which drove me crazy. I think that Carter thought of the fever as a just outcome from the fight that I had put an end to. Brent would have gotten better sooner had he stayed in bed, but Brent being Brent meant that the opposite was true. I could honestly say that I dreaded ever going through that process all over again if Brent got sick a second time before the summer was out.

"Thank God!" I sagged with relief just as Joshua walked into the room.

"What?"

"Brent is officially without fever." Joshua offered a smile my way.

"Of course I'm without fever. I've been trying to tell you that this whole week!" Brent glared at me, to which I rolled my eyes. I was not about to be pulled back into that argument again.

"Well, just so you know, the library's done."
I turned my head around to face Joshua so quickly, I almost got whiplash.

"What do you mean?"

"Just what I said."

"Joshua." I wasn't as amused as he was.

"No, I mean what I said. I just visited it, and it looks spotless."

"Are you kidding?" Brent chimed in, and Joshua gave a sigh of exasperation.

"No! If you two don't believe me, just go check yourselves!" I jumped to my feet and reached behind me to pull Brent along, knowing that he wouldn't come as fast if I didn't.

Strange things had been happening, and I was only just now fully realizing them. This past week hadn't just revolved around Brent's fever. One day I had woken up to find that my mural had been magically extended to cover all of my walls, not just the living room wall. It was stunning! All of the other details were smaller, but there was an ornate stone railing along the majority of the staircases, the walls were smoother, and something about the atmosphere was different. Maybe it was just the lighting from the torches, which had also become brighter as well, but there was a warmth everywhere that replaced the coolness from before.

All of these things were honestly starting to put me on edge. It felt like the calm before the storm. Part of me wished my mom could be here with me. She would know what was wrong... I jolted myself out of that train of thought. If I got stuck

233

thinking about home, I would never stop. I had written them a letter, but, as I expected, I hadn't obtained reply. I didn't even know if they had ever received it. I had to pull myself out of my thoughts again.

"Wow."

Both Brent and I came to a stop at the library entrance.

"Please tell me: Did the library look this clean when you first came here." This I had to know.

"Uh, yeah. It did. It looked pretty much the same as this." All that told me was that he was responsible for the mess that the library had been before.

Both of us began to tour the room. I took two steps before looking down to see why my bare feet didn't feel freezing cold stone.

"The floor is made of wood."

"That's new."

"No way." I continued walking, only to see Brent reach out a hand towards a bookshelf. "Hey! Don't start shifting books yet!" Brent scowled at me, but pulled his hand back. I made sure to turn away before I began to giggle.

"And just why do you think you're laughing?" I looked over my shoulder and smiled disarmingly.

"No reason."

"Liar." I only smiled more widely and continued to make my way past the shelves.

Every once in a while there were small corners or spaces that held a chair or two for hiding away with a novel. After a couple of minutes of walking, I realized that I hadn't reached the end of the library yet.

"Brent, is it just me, or does the library seem to be a whole lot larger than before?"

"That's because it is." I turned around for more explanation. "Every couple of months, the library expands or shrinks. It just expanded, meaning that all of these books here will be slightly different than before."

I liked the idea of searching for the answer to the curse with a whole new perspective. No wonder he hadn't been searching in earnest before I joined in on the hunt. He had already gone through the entire library. It did explain the giant book piles everywhere.

I glanced over at a couple of nearby books.

"Well, I'm almost positive these books won't help." I pulled one of them out and flipped it open. "Look!" I held it up for Brent to see some of the diagrams inside. "It shows you how to do ballroom dancing."

"Hmmm." He didn't look too interested. Maybe I could solve that.

"Dance with me!" I gave him my best angelic look as he stared back like a deer caught in headlights.

"No, thank you." He politely declined.

"Oh, come on! It'll be easy." He didn't look thrilled at all, and I was having a hard time keeping a straight face.

"I don't dance."

"That doesn't mean you can't." Brent looked as though he was honestly contemplating my words for a moment before he deadpanned.

"No." Well, that got nowhere. I wouldn't tell Brent, but I hadn't expected to actually dance with him. I knew that he would refuse, no matter what.

I looked at the book in my hands.

"I wonder if the books still reshelf themselves," I mused before chucking it at Brent frisbee style. Brent jerked back at the sudden movement, but, once again, the book missed him as it flew back to its spot of the shelf.

"Alli..." I giggled at the way he said my name. "Do you really find that necessary?"

"Yes." I smiled widely.

Eventually we settled down in a random corner. There was only one chair, but Brent seemed perfectly content to sit on the floor and lean against it.

"Whatcha reading?" I leaned over the arm of the chair and peeked over his shoulder. Brent closed the book before turning his head so that we faced each other.

"Wouldn't you like to know?"

"Yes. Yes, I would." I suddenly realized how close our faces were and froze. Were his eyes always that green? The warm feeling was back, and it filled my body with a sense of safety, protection, and something else I wasn't sure about yet. We really were close enough to... I jerked my mind away from the thought before I could finish it.

236

"Fine, don't tell me." I smoothly pulled myself into a sitting position once more, focusing on anywhere but Brent. The silence was fairly awkward after that moment; at least it was to me. I wondered if he even knew what almost happened. I was doing my best to stop the blush from trailing up my cheeks, but my attempts weren't working very well.

The 'lights out' time could not come fast enough.

~*~

"Yes. Yes, I would." Brent felt as though her words had put him in a trance. He couldn't move as he watched Alli's eyes fill with realization, curiosity, warmth, shock, and then embarrassment before they went blank. "Fine, don't tell me."

Alli's attention went back to the book in her lap, but Brent was still frozen.

Had she-they almost... No. She wouldn't. She didn't. He was fool to think that even for a moment she...

No. He could not let himself be tricked by his own feelings that would never be returned.

The horrible silence was returning between them, and he hated it with a passion. He had let this happen.

He should have known this would happen.
He should have known.

Chapter 17

I needed a breather; some night air to sort out my feelings.

Brent had been closing me off ever since that moment in the library, and it was all my fault. I could see the hurt and pain in his eyes, but only barely. The cold mask that he used to put up to guard his emotions when I first came was returning. I had never realized how easy it was to feel comfortable in his presence until recently, but now...

Aside from not knowing how to feel about Brent anymore, I felt emotionally beaten in every other regard. I felt desperate to see my mom and brother, and though I knew that the summer was almost over, I couldn't stand not knowing how they were. All I had was the occasional reassurance from Brent that they were doing fine, but knowing that he couldn't leave this place made me wonder if he really knew, or if he was just trying to keep me calm. I trusted him. But still...

The wind was strong that night as it whipped my hair around. I couldn't see any clouds, but I wouldn't be surprised if there was a storm brewing by the morning. Chills ran down my spine, even though it was a warm night.

In spite of my best efforts, tears formed in my eyes. I wanted to go home so badly. How much longer would this summer last?

"Alli?" I let out a soft gasp, turning around. Brent stood about ten feet away, a concerned look on his face. I quickly turned back to the sea and tried to wipe away the tears from my face, but he had already seen them. "What's wrong?"

"Nothing." My voice was too strained. It was obvious I was lying through my teeth. I felt a warm hand on my shoulder, but I refused to look his way. I tried to distract him. "It's beautiful." I gestured toward the sea.

"Yes." He knew what I was doing.

"The view reminds me of that dance I tried to get you to do a week ago. This would be a great place to dance if there was music." I was rambling.

"You don't need music to dance." Brent was humoring me. I shrugged my shoulders. "I'll show you." Brent pulled me to him, and I felt heat rush to my face.

"You mean, you want to dance now?" He gave a low chuckle, and I let out a puff of annoyance. "Why couldn't you have been this willing a week ago?" Still, I put my hand on his shoulder and he slid a hand around my waist. He began to move to the steps of the dance, and I looked down at the ground, doing my best to not step on his feet.

"Just look up. Follow my lead and you won't mess up." Maybe now wasn't the best time to tell him that I had never danced with a guy before, and I was sure that I couldn't dance well at all.

"When did you learn how to dance?" I tried to tease him into stopping before I humiliated myself.

"Not long ago." Brent didn't really answer my question. "Just look up."

My face was sure to be flaming red right now. Nevertheless, I looked up at his scarred face, and he pulled me closer, somehow making it easier to follow his steps. My thoughts were racing a thousand miles a minute. I had never seen him look at me that way before.

It was a slow dance, and a small memory suddenly awoke in my mind. It was of a time many years ago, when my father wasn't so messed-up. He was bending down, holding my small five-year-old hands in his and twirling me around like a princess. What really struck me was the light in his eyes. He looked happy and loving.

Tear filled my eyes and I squeezed them shut, lowering my head. Brent's arms came around me, and I sobbed into his chest. For a long time, we stood there like that, until my tears came to a slow stop.

When I pulled away, Brent lead me over to the edge of the cliff and sat down with me.

"What's the matter?" His voice broke the silence of the night softly.

"I'm sorry-I--I like it here, I really do. I don't really understand, but for the first time in many years I feel safe and happy, but, still...I miss them so

241

much." I spoke the last part quietly. I took a deep, shaky breath and looked out at the distant town. "How do you know? How do you know that my family is safe, if you can't leave this place?"

I glanced at Brent to see if he was angry that I was basically saying that I wanted out of my deal early...again. After a long period of silence, I opened my mouth to try to take back my words, but Brent suddenly stood up.

"Brent?" I really hoped that he wasn't going to leave me alone out of anger. I thought that he had gotten over doing that a long time ago.

"I need to show you something." There was a sorrow in his voice that I had never heard before. He helped me stand up and held my hand as he led me to the portal. Once inside, he led me through the dark, up some stairs, through another door, and up some more stairs.

There were torches that lit up the room, and although it had changed, I recognized it as Brent's room. I stared at the door where the rose was held, until Brent pulled me towards a different door. He grabbed a torch from the wall and went through the door, closing it behind us. It led to a small room where a large mirror with a thin golden frame sat, leaning against the wall.

If I didn't trust Brent, I would be freaked out. The room had a dark feel to it. In the stone walls, there were several long gouges at random places. I took a small step closer to Brent.

"What is this place?" My words felt suppressed, as though the air was thicker.

"If you wish to see something or someone, this mirror can show you." I stared at the mirror. All the reflection showed was my small figure, standing next to Brent's larger, scarred one. I was amazed at the look that I saw reflected in Brent's eyes. They looked haunted and tired, but also open, as though he was being completely vulnerable at that very moment. "Just tell the mirror what you wish to see." I took a deep breath.

"Show me my mother." I wondered if this thing really worked.

The glass reflection fogged up, and a brief second later, I could see my mom, sitting at the kitchen table. She held a mug in her hands, but ignored it as she staring out of the window. The mirror zoomed out on the area around her, and I could see that there were others with her.

A man slammed his fists onto the tabletop, and I jumped when I realized I could hear the noise.

"Just tell us where she is!" I let out a gasp. I knew that voice. It belonged to one of the men that had almost killed Brent when he was shot with the gun. Rasp.

"I already told you. I don't know where my daughter is. She's away for the summer." It was scary how hollow Mom's voice sounded. There was a loud crash from somewhere out of the line of my sight, and both of them looked toward the sound.

I could hear muffled sound of someone shouting for someone to let go, and I unconsciously moved closer to Brent.

My mom's eyes came alive at that moment, suddenly much sharper than before.

"Let him go! My son has no part in our discussion!" A strangled noise came from the back of my throat. The scene zoomed out some more, and I could suddenly see my brother. He was taller and tanner than I last remembered, but I had to remind myself that I hadn't seen him for the whole summer. He was being held by some other man, and there was an anger in his eyes that I hadn't seen before.

"If nothing will get your attention, then maybe this will. If you want to see your son again, tell me where that daughter of yours is and her useless father!"

The scene disappeared from the mirror, leaving just my reflection once more. My knees gave out and Brent caught me before I hit the ground. I buried my face in his chest as a few tears flowed from my eyes.

"What am I going to do? I have to find them! I-" I began to pull away from Brent, but he put his hands on my shoulders and forced me to look at him.

"Then go to them." I blinked, not fully understanding the weight of his words.

"You mean-"

"Yes! They need you, so go!" He spoke more forcefully and I took a step in the direction of the door, hesitating. "Go!"

I turned around and threw myself into his arms, hugging him tightly. "Thank you!" I didn't trust myself to say anything else and pulled away, practically running out of the room. I found myself soon standing on the road outside. I took a moment to figure out the direction of town and took off at a run.

I never thought that I would be leaving that place unwillingly. A part of me would always be there. It's funny how life works like that.

~*~

"Yes! They need you, so go!" Brent's words tasted bitter in his own mouth. "Go!"

When Alli hugged him one last time, he held onto her as though he never wanted to let her go. He didn't.

"Thank you!" Her soft, broken voice whispered so quietly that he could barely hear her, and then she was gone. He felt as though his heart would break.

Brent stared at the empty doorway for a moment before running out of it, trying to get to the cliffside. He made it there just in time to see her form disappear around one of the bends in the road.

"Go." He whispered one last time, before he sank to his knees.

"So you let her go." Would the enchantress never leave him alone?

"Yes." His words were empty. "She was never mine to begin with. It was foolish of me to even try to keep her here."

"Do you regret it then?"

"Yes."

"You would go back and change the fact that she came here if you could?"

"Never."

"And why is that?" Brent finally looked into her eyes.

"How can I regret falling in love?"

~*~

I could feel my body tiring after only a couple of minutes, and I suddenly began to wish that I had taken some sort of sport last year. My endurance was pitiful, but I kept going. Someone was bound to come along who would give me a ride.

Just as the thought crossed my mind, a familiar dark red car pulled up alongside me, and the window rolled down to reveal Carter's welcome face.

"Hop in!" He unlocked the car, and I slid in the front seat.

"Hurry!" I gasped. "Take me home!"

Carter did as I said, but he gave me a strange look. "Why are you leaving?" There was desperation in his voice.

I told him what I had seen in the mirror, as I recovered my breath. When I finished, Carter stayed silent, but I did notice that the car had picked up momentum. We were going several miles over the speed limit, so I though it wise to not distract Carter as he drove.

The trip coming to the cliffside had taken about an hour, but Carter managed to cut that time in half by speeding and going through several backstreets. I have no idea how we managed to avoid getting a ticket.

By the time we reached a familiar street, I could no longer see the night sky. It was hidden behind a veil of clouds, and I could barely see a thing.

We were about ten minutes away, when I saw car headlights in front of us, and I did one of the most stupid things I'd ever done. I had Carter slam on the brakes, and I jumped out of my seat, right into the other car's pathway. I waved my hands, shouting for it to stop. Stupid was an understatement. The car skidded to stop not five feet from me, and the driver jerked open his door and got out.

"Are you crazy?! I almost killed you! What-"

"Please, sir! I need a phone!" I tried to cut the man off. "It's a matter of life and death!"

"Lady-"

"Please! I need the police!" My voice cracked dangerously and a small bead of sweat trickled down the back of my neck. The man suddenly looked concerned.

"Hey, what's wrong? Is someone after you?"

"No. Yes. They're threatening my mom and brother. Now, may I have a phone?" This was taking forever, but the man snapped into action and pulled out his phone, handing it to me. I dialed 911 and waited for someone to pick-up.

"9-1-1, what's your-" I cut the woman who answered off.

"Please, I need help! There are men holding my brother captive and threatening my mom!"

247

"Where are you?" I gave her the address of my home and cut off the phone call.

"Thanks!" I shoved the phone into the guy's hand and got back in the car with Carter. Carter quickly started down the road again, leaving the poor man behind, looking completely baffled.

He took as many shortcuts he knew, and we soon heard sirens and saw the lights of police cars pass us. Almost there!

I had Carter park about two blocks away so that he wouldn't be mistaken for my kidnapper. The last time my mom saw him, it wasn't exactly the best of situations. I got out of the car and ran the rest of the way to my house.

Life can be strange sometimes. It's in the moments where you trip over a large stone and are grabbed in the dark right before you manage to get to safety when you start to wonder where you went wrong.

A strong hand covered my mouth, and I was pulled away from the light of the police cars. I briefly wondered how the police would react if they knew I had been kidnapped literally twenty feet away from them, and they didn't even know it. I mentally cursed my luck. I knew that Carter was just far enough away to not be able to see me.

I was pulled down the street about a block away from both the police and Carter before I heard the screech of metal. The ground disappeared from under my feet as I was thrown into the back of a storage truck. The breath was temporarily knocked out of me, and as I struggled for air, a flashlight clicked on, shining brightly in my eyes. I held up a hand against it.

"Think you're so clever, eh?" A rough hand grabbed the back on my neck, and I was forced to look into the eyes of my captor. I recognized him as the same man I had seen holding my brother; Brute is the name I decided to give him. Brute kept speaking. "Calling the police like that?" I tried to jerk away, but his fingers dug into the sides of my neck, hitting a painful pressure point. I gave a small cry in pain and arched my back against the pressure.

"Wha-what do you want?" I gasped.

"First, we are going to figure out what you and that demon friend of your's know, then..." I saw a dangerous gleam in his eyes as he trailed off, and a shiver ran down my spine. I was in so much trouble.

"But, duty first." I heard the quiet, rough voice of Sile. I had so hoped that he had been killed the night Brent had been shot. "Our first priority is to figure out what her father told her."

I immediately knew that they wouldn't believe anything I said. They must think that my father had told me something that neither of us was supposed to know, and that I told Brent.

"My friend doesn't know anything!" I winced internally at how pathetic I sounded.

Brute let up on the pressure on my neck, and I gulped in air like a starving man. "Too late, our colleague went ahead to go chat with your friend." He grinned eerily in the dark and began to cut off

249

my oxygen supply again. "He should be much easier to handle by now." He must be talking about Rasp.

Before Brute could say anything else, there was a loud thud from behind him. A moment later, there was another muffled thunk and his iron grip on my neck disappeared as both of us went limp on the ground. I did my absolute best to scoot away from his body as the pain drained from my body.

"Are you okay?" A familiar voice spoke in the darkness.

"Carter!" I picked myself up off of the floor and threw myself at him, hugging him fiercely before pulling back. "How did you know?" I could still see his eyes roll, even though there was barely any light whatsoever.

"I followed you by foot." He made it sound as though he was doing the most natural thing in the world by following me. "Do you really think you could slip away without one of us making sure you were safe?" That was exactly what I had thought.

"Brent!" I gasped suddenly. Something that the man had said finally registered in my brain.

"What?" Carter gave me a strange look. "I'm Carter."

"We have to go! Brent's in trouble! They sent someone ahead!" I'm sure that Carter was completely confused, but he didn't ask questions.

"Follow me." Carter led me out of the storage truck and to the car. The sky had finally begun to let loose some drops of rain, and thunder rolled across the sky.

When Carter tried to turn the key in the engine, it took three tries before the car started up. That couldn't have been a good sign. Carter must have agreed, because his body tensed up, and he immediately turned the car around. He was definitely going wildly over the speed limit. I really hoped he knew what he was doing. I didn't feel like dying just yet.

I gripped the handle on the door as neighborhoods and streets went by in a flash. The trip took even less time than before, but it still felt like an eternity had passed by the time the cliff came into view. The car was shuddering violently when Carter pulled to a stop. I ripped the door open, bracing myself against the strong winds, and ran to the cliff wall.

"Help me find the opening!" I shouted over the howl of the wind, and Carter began a search of his own to find it.

"Got it!" I could barely hear Carter in the darkness. A huge clap of thunder sounded above us as we pushed through the rock and out of the storm. I ran to the dim light of the bonfire and found the once large flames had been reduced to dying embers. The rain from outside was coming through the window, forming a large, spreading puddle.

"Brent!" I yelled into the darkness, desperately hoping that he wasn't outside.

"Alli? Where were you?! We thought-" I could hear Joshua's voice in the dark, coming from the general direction of his room, but I cut him off.

"Where is Brent?!"

251

"He never came back in from outside once you left!" Joshua finally came running into the room, but I ignored him and ran past him. If he was outside, then Joshua and Carter couldn't reach him. I stumbled up the steps until I found the portal.

Whatever clothing on me that wasn't already soaked certainly was soaked now as chilling rain lashed against my skin.

Lightning lit up the sky for a moment, and I lurched forward at the sight of two figures close to the cliff edge.

"Brent!" I tried to shout, but my voice was drowned out by the thunder that followed the lightning. I tripped at the sound and scrambled to get back to my feet, running towards Brent. "Brent!" Lightning flashed again, and I saw his eyes wide, staring at me.

"Alli! Get out of her-" Thunder rolled. Even though the thunder was deafening, it still couldn't block the sound of the gunshot. I screamed as Brent lurched to his knees. It was an all too familiar scene. Fury built up inside of me, and I threw the best punch I could, which in my book was pretty good. The guy mostly slipped on wet grass, but it was enough for him to lose the grip on his gun, and it slipped off of the cliff. I felt decently proud. I fell to my knees next to Brent, ignoring my now throbbing hand.

"Brent! Please tell me you're alright!" If he heard me, I couldn't tell. His face was twisted with pain.

"Get out of here!"

"Not without you!" I was pulling his arm over my shoulder as I spoke, but then I looked up and a slightly strangled sound escaped my throat. Lightning flashed, and the edge of a knife barely missed my face as Brent's arm tightened around my shoulder and pulled me backwards.

I landed in the grass with enough force to knock the air out of me. I desperately choked to get air into my lungs and wiped rain from my eyes to see what was happening.

Brent was directly in front of me on one knee, pushing the killer back. How long he could last while being shot, I didn't know. The knife in the killer's hand quivered with the force that the man gripped it with. With a large shove, Brent managed to force him onto his back with him on top. This unfortunately gave just enough leeway to the killer to plunge the knife into Brent's side.

"No!" I choked on the word as I struggled to sit up. Brent let out a strangled cry that seemed to twist something inside my chest painfully. The killer shoved Brent to the side, but to my amazement, Brent latched onto the man, preventing him from getting far. With one large jerk, Brent wrenched the man over the side of the cliff, sliding half off in the process himself.

I threw myself forward and wrapped an arm around him to stop the momentum from carrying him over the edge.

"No, no, no, no, Brent! Come on, stay with me!" I carefully rolled him onto his back. His eyes were shut in pain and he was struggling to breath. I

253

applied pressure with my hands to the bullet entrance in his chest and looked at the knife still in his side with despair. "You can't leave me!" My voice broke as tears streamed down my face. "Please don't leave me! Brent! Open your eyes!"

"Alli. We have got to...stop getting into these situations." I could barely hear him as I looked at him with wide, despairing eyes. His whole body shuddered, and a sob wrenched itself from my chest. He didn't say anything for the longest time, before he whispered again, "Alli."

"I'm here!" I tried my best to see any movement in his chest, but I couldn't see anything. "Please stay with me! You can make it!"

"Alli." His eyes opened briefly, barely focusing on my face.

"I'm here!" I whispered, bending my head closer.

"I..." Another shuddering breath. "I love you." Lightning lit up the sky above.

And just like that, he shut his eyes and went still. Thunder rolled.

"Brent? Brent!" I was reeling from his confession. He loved me. "Don't- You can't die!" That horrible word finally came out of my mouth and I broke down completely, barely able to breath. After all this time, I finally understood what that warm feeling was that I got whenever I was near Brent. "I love you, too."

He was gone.

After several minutes, I could feel a warm arm around my shoulders, a stark contrast to the cold body beneath me. I wanted nothing more than to ignore it, but another arm helped pull me away from Brent.

"Please." I sobbed. Why couldn't the person leave me alone?

"Shhh. Alli, it's going to be alright." I blinked hard to see through my tears. There was a tall, slender woman kneeling on the grass with a soft, knowing smile on her face. I took me a little bit, but I realized that she wasn't wet. Her long dark hair moved softly in the air, even though the storm raged on around us.

"Who-who are you?" My words felt muffled in the wind as thunder cracked again.

The woman just smiled at me and stood up. She was wearing a simple white dress that seemed to glow in the darkness. I shivered as a strong burst of wind suddenly lashed at my body, causing me to fall back farther from Brent's body. The woman knelt next to him and pulled the dagger out of his side.

"Mark, it's not quite your time yet." Why did she call him Mark? I was going to ask, but I gasped and covered my mouth with my hand as Brent's eyes fluttered open. Something was different about him.

He let out a loud groan as though in pain and his back arched. I watched with disbelief as he changed before my very eyes. As the rain fell, the water ran down his body and left behind perfect, unblemished skin. The scars had disappeared His shoulders weren't as broad and his clothes seemed looser, but he still seemed to be mostly the same person. His hair grew much longer, as though he hadn't cut it in a long time, and the light brown hair fell almost to his shoulders in the rain.

When the changes stopped, Brent's body suddenly relaxed, going limp.

"Brent?" I whispered his name softly, and his eyes shot open. As he slowly sat up, I suddenly realized what the woman had meant. "Mark?" There was no way, but... "How?" I was so confused. Brent was Mark, and Mark was Brent. The same Brent that I had fallen for, and the same Mark who had hated me.

"Alli?" His voice was still the same. New tears formed in my eyes.

"Is it true? You're really Mark? The same Mark who enjoyed hurting me?" I didn't know what to believe anymore.

"I am." My shoulders slumped. "But," he continued, "I'm also the same Mark who was cursed, who became Brent, and who changed when he fell in love with you." I looked up at him when I felt his warm hand touch the side of my face almost cautiously. He was staring back at me with his green eyes. The same green eyes I had always known. "I still love you." He looked as though he was desperate for me to believe him.

"Promise?" I whispered, barely able to get the words through the knot in my throat.

"Promise."

I threw myself into his arms, which wrapped around me and held me. The same warmth that I had always gotten around Brent filled me. I pulled back slightly to look at him directly. "I love you, too."

Then, finally, as rain poured down around us, he kissed me. I felt as though I could feel the electricity in the lightning above course through me. It was everything I had imagined a real kiss to be like and more. The thunder seemed to agree as it sealed the moment.

Perfect.

Epilogue

1 month later

"Come on. Come on." I muttered, bouncing on the balls of my feet, looking around for any sign of him.

"Guess who?" Large hands suddenly blocked my vision. I smirked before turning around.

"Hello, Mark." He raised an eyebrow.

"You know the point is to guess who I am before turning around."

"You mean I've been playing the game wrong all along?" Mark narrowed his eyes.

"You've been hanging out with Carter too much." I just smiled before grabbing his hand and pulling him along.

"Come on! We'll be late for the first day!"

"We won't be late!"

"Your definition and my definition of late are two very different things." I said dryly, but I slowed down anyway. I felt as though I could finally relax with him nearby. Things were still hard, but Mark had so far proved to be a solid pillar in my life.

259

The past month had proved to be testing. When the curse was broken, all of the magic attached to it had disappeared as well. The entire inside of the cliff home had condensed, growing smaller and smaller. Joshua and Carter had barely gotten out in time. The portals were gone as well, and it was only because of the Enchantress that Mark and I had gotten down the cliff side without going through the state park. It was the first time in almost two years that Mark had been outside the cliff home, and the look in his eyes told me how happy he was to leave it behind.

The one thing that surprised me was how hard it was to return home. Of course, my mom and brother were thrilled beyond belief that I was back, but then my mom's health began to fail. It was nowhere near as bad as it was before, but she still needed more sleep than normal. It broke my heart to think that she still had to go through this sickness. She was at least able to work again.

As for my father, no one knows where he is right now, and there was still a warrant out for his arrest. Out of his old associates, Rasp and Creep were both killed, while Sile and Brute were both arrested the night the curse broke, thanks to Carter. Both were unconscious when found, due to head injuries. The police told us that they belonged to some type of crime ring that specialized in blackmail material. Apparently, my father had discovered something while working with them that they didn't want him to know, so he made a run for it. When they tried to get ahold of him, he was already long gone, so they had come to his family, thinking he may have told us something about where he was and/or what he knew.

I shuddered at the memories and pulled myself back to present day. I had secured an after-school job that consumed most of my time, but any extra time I had, I spent with Mark.

"Have you spoken to your parents yet?" I asked Mark softly. He gave me a small, strained smile. Mark had told me that he had crashed at his grandparents' place on his dad's side of the family. They had been surprised and concerned to find that Mark needed a place to stay, but they were more than willing to provide it. They didn't know a thing about the past two years. Apparently, Mark's parents weren't very close to them and hadn't made an effort to tell them that Mark had been missing.

"I contacted them yesterday."

"And?" I got a bad feeling in my stomach.

"And nothing. They thought I had gone to some distant relatives in another state. They didn't care. To be honest, I don't think they ever did. I mean, both of them always worked and I rarely saw them. I've always been more of a bother than their son." I squeezed his hand.

"I'm so sorry." I bit my lip. What should I say about that? At least my mom was a constant in my life. "Well, look on the bright side! You have me!" I gave him a grin, inwardly congratulating myself when he cracked a smile. I decided that it was time to change the subject.

"Where are Joshua and Carter?"

Brent hadn't been the only one to change. I was a little shocked to find out that both Joshua and Carter were also around my age. Apparently, the magic had made them appear older out of necessity for their job.

The enchantress had given them assignments for the past two years where they would be in the right places at the right times to help people. Sometimes, this meant just changing a flat tire on an empty road, while other times, it meant fixing something that someone couldn't afford to repair. They were sort of like guardian angels in that sense, but I had a hard time think about them as angels without smiling after knowing them personally.

"Joshua's probably already at school, but as for Carter..." Brent tried to look ahead farther up the sidewalk and obviously found what he was looking for because he turned to me with a sigh of exasperation. "Carter's scaring some poor girl by trying to flirt with her." I giggled as soon as I saw the girl Brent was talking about. I recognized her from last year.

"Don't worry about her. I'm more worried for him. He has no idea what he's getting himself into.

"Oh?" We both watched as the girl looked directly into Carter's eyes and spoke for about ten seconds before walking away. I don't know what she said, but it obviously startled Carter, because he stared after her with his mouth agape. After several seconds of him looking confused, he shook his head and gave a dopey looking grin in her general direction. He looked absolutely smitten.

Mark and I cracked up laughing and kept walking hand and hand toward the school entrance. As we passed a girl rising from her spot under a tree, I heard a startled gasp. This similar situation happened several times before I finally recalled that about half of the school hadn't seen Mark in two years. Everyone had known how much he hated me before he left, so seeing us holding hands would be a shocker. I could already feel the rumors building around us.

"I see that you are causing quite the stir here." Joshua appeared out of nowhere next to us, hands lazily in his pockets.

"Yep." I smiled up at Brent. "I have a feeling this will be one crazy school year." Joshua laughed at the new understatement of the year. I squeezed Brent's hand, and he squeezed back as we both walked through the school door. It would be crazy, probably stressful, but awesome.

I felt ready for anything.

"But I am not concerned with any of the separate statutes of elfland, but with the whole spirit of its law, which I learnt before I could speak, and shall retain when I cannot write. I am concerned with a certain way of looking at life, which was created in me by the fairy tales, but has since been meekly ratified by the mere facts." [3]

-G. K. Chesterton, Orthodoxy

Endnotes

1. Shakespeare, William. "Macbeth: Act 1. Scene 1."
   William Shakespeare: The Complete Works. New
   York: Barnes and Noble, 1994. N. pag. Print.
2. The Complete Fairy Tales of the Brothers Grimm
   translated by Jack Zipes, Bantam Books 1992
3. Chesterton, G. K. Orthodoxy. Chicago: Moody, 2009.
   Print.

Acknowledgements

First off, I want to thank my family for putting up with me as I struggled to get this book published. I don't know what I would do without you. Dad, for being the entire reason that I got hooked on fairytales and fantasy when he bought me *The Sisters Grimm: The Fairy Tale Detectives* by Michael Buckley. Mom, for giving continual support and constantly urging me to finish, even when I didn't want to write. Thank you, also, for helping me polish up the final draft, so that it looked even better than before. Ella and Samantha- thank you both for being the best sisters in the whole world, devouring this story, and giving me the confidence that other people would enjoy it as much as you two.

Next, are some of the greatest people in the world (in my humble opinion). Lily Wendt, who is the person completely responsible for me becoming a writer. She invited me to read one of her stories and join a writing group, and, from that point on, I wrote. Catherine Anderson, for being an amazing writing partner/encouragement as we both figured out how to tell good stories. Ashlyn Thompson, for being an awesome friend and grammar guru as she listened to my many complaints about the writing process. Also, one big shout out to all those who read and critiqued early drafts of *Rose* and made it a better fairytale for years to come.

I want to also thank Melissa Marmor for being the greatest and most patient editor in the world. She made time for this story, even though her schedule was already crazy, and tediously went through it, always coming back with helpful comment and suggestions. I cringe to think of how this book might have turned out without her.

Finally, I want to thank Victoria Presley, who made it possible for me to use my own art for the cover. Thank you for answering my numerous questions and complaints about confusing technology, even when you didn't have the time!

Thank you all for being the most wonderful people to grace the earth with your presence and for making such a difference in my life!

About the Author

Madeline Simpkins was born and raised in the great city of Austin, Texas. She has read an alarming number of books growing up, and still does to this day. This is the first book she has written, which she completed at the age of 16, as a junior in High School. In her mind, the best day in the world would include a good book, a blanket, and a hot cup of tea.

Made in the USA
Middletown, DE
02 February 2017